Front cover illustration, **Shineta Horton, 2023**

Urban Tales for Beginners
The Time Bandit From Nubia
© 2023 N.M. Shabazz. All Rights Reserved.
ISBN#9798885677028
Printed in the United States of America.
For more information:
Blackhistoryforbeginners@gmail.com
Spoken History Education and Publishing Services
Kansas City, Missouri 64129

For bookclub information, please visit
www.facebook.com/historyforbeginners or e-mail
Blackhistoryforbeginners@gmail.com to join our
distribution list.

First Edition July 2023

The Time Bandit from Nubia

N.M. Shabazz

Contents

Dedication

May 18th, 2023

Dear Laura Partridge:

You used to sit across the table from me at night and read the words as they came out of the printer. You asked questions, telling me what didn't make sense and what I needed to clarify. I was surprised that sometimes you hung on every word. I don't know if you realize what your actions meant.

I was asphyxiating and you breathed life into me; I was drowning and you pulled me up from the depths of the sea. While I write because it's in my blood, it's a pleasure to know that what I am creating is worth someone's time. It was a pleasure to know my writing was worth YOUR time. While we may not be at the same place we were, spiritually the bond has never been broken and I hope it never will be.

You could have shared your life with anyone else in the world. Instead, you chose to share it with a wild, unorganized idealist like me. Overstand this: There would be no Black History for Beginners series without you; I would have abandoned the project a long time ago had it not been for your enthusiasm.

You became my muse. You ARE my muse, part of my motivation. I hope you read this book and laugh and cry like we used to do and remember me like I remember you.

Always your friend,

N.M. Shabazz

Acknowledgements

This novel is a little unusual because it is, to some degree, a history book. In fact, despite it being a science fiction novel about time travel, the history presented is very real. This is one of the reasons a bibliography is provided in the back. I want readers to understand I didn't just pull concepts or elements out of thin air.

There is no Critical Race Theory (CRT) debate or any of that political hullabaloo. I just present the characters and story like my father always presented life to me, straight up with no chaser. Additionally, since I am a secondary education teacher—social studies and geography—there are academic questions and exercises in the back related to the themes presented in the book, one of which is creating your very own *Return to Nubia*.

With all the above said, I have to acknowledge some of the forces and people who influenced me while writing *The Time Bandit From Nubia*. The two HBCUs from which I graduated, the University of Arkansas Pine Bluff and Langston University, gave me a deep understanding of Afrocentrism and the concepts surrounding it. These two institutions, and the professors who worked there and who continue to mentor me, are a big influence on my life.

Before attending Langston University in 1988, I

had never heard of things like the **Tulsa Race Massacre** or of people like Bass Reeves. I left both institutions more aware and prepared for life. Yet there is now a new force in my life and I welcome the addition! My paranoia in beginning doctoral school at Saint Louis University had nothing to do with thinking I couldn't complete the program and everything to do with thinking academic writing would destroy my creativity. I am glad to say it appears my fears were unwarranted.

If anything, the interaction with my professors, their grilling and pushing me to dig deeper for understanding, has increased my creativity and made my writing better. *Who would have thunk it?* I sincerely and profusely want to thank them all, particularly Dr. Mandy Wood!

Another force or, better yet, a person who has been an asset and continues to be an influence in my life, is my mentor, Dr. Lester Blue. When I started my Black History for Beginners series, he selflessly offered editing and creative advice. He has never asked for a penny, only for more knowledge to expand his already expansive mind state. I wanted him to know I appreciate his presence in my life.

Chapter One
the philosophy of disbelief

Until yesterday, I believed the question to be purely philosophical. If you could go back in time and change the past, would you? Of course, the offer IS tempting. To play God. To act in what one deems the best interest of mankind—in MY best interest— changing the mistakes humans have made.

I mean, what rational person WOULDN'T want to alter errors? Marriage only lasted a couple of years and ended up in divorce? Fine. Go back in time and change what went wrong or never marry in the first place. A person could focus on something entirely different, though. Many despicable or insidious beings existed in the past, like Adolph Hitler.

Who wouldn't jump at the chance to go back and slit his throat? What, too much? Don't play bleeding heart liberal with me! I'm talking about World War II and preventing millions of deaths and ethnic genocide. Being a history professor, the time travel question in and of itself is a perplexing conundrum.

Then I think about what people SMARTER than I have said about the subject if time travel were possible. The most anyone SHOULD do is observe and not interfere with any physical aspect of the past. If a person DID change it, the present would still come true in some form or fashion. Destiny and the will of God cannot be altered.

However, attempting to do so might transform things into something invariably worse. If a person went back in time and killed Hitler, a similar demagogue would eventually come to power to produce the same death and destruction worldwide. Sometimes it is better to be familiar with the devil one knows than the one who is unfamiliar.

Thinking about it again, I probably WOULDN'T go back in time, despite my profession. Having made my career analyzing the past, I would be too tempted to change some of it. Anyway, what did it matter? As I said, until yesterday the question was purely philosophical. But now...

***

"Pretend you're talking to a 15-year-old and repeat that to me, please," I said in disbelief, attempting not to laugh. Despite the whirlwind nature of the last 24 hours—people busting into my house, me being whisked away in secrecy to Area 51 and now standing in a room full of high-ranking military personnel—I couldn't take what I had heard seriously.

Thomas, the scientist who stood in front of me, had been assigned to explain things, but even he appeared to be a joke. If ever there was a funny-looking, White male adult Steve Erkel, it was him. He seemed as nervous and as impatient as I.

In attempting to sympathize, I was still sure someone was pulling an elaborate joke. He took his time and tried to rephrase his verbiage.

"Okay, let me be more direct, Dr. Mazique," he retorted, putting more bass in his voice, "the United States military has developed the ability to manipulate the timestream." He pointed to the enormous monstrosity of a machine around which everyone seemed to be crowded.

"Although we were still in the experimental phases, unauthorized military personnel used it to enter the stream."

WTF? I STILL didn't believe anything he was saying. "What do you mean, they used it to enter the stream?"

"I meant just that. They took an unauthorized trip into the past. We believe they mean to change it."

The question slipped out of my mouth loud enough to be heard. "Is that even possible?"

"Yes, it's possible," Thomas uttered, trying to be sarcastic or witty; I still haven't decided which. "I just told you; the military has developed a machine that allows users to enter the timestream."

I gave Thomas the stank eye. I thought to myself, *Get smart with me again and I'm gonna hit you in the throat.* Instead, I calmly replied, "I didn't ask you to get flippant, millennial. I simply asked for clarification."

Taken aback by my rhetoric, his eyes widened. "I didn't mean any offense."

I smiled while continuing to give him an evil look.

"And I don't mean any offense when I ask this question again. Is this a joke? Someone PLEASE tell me it is. Before all of this, I was sitting at my dinner table about to enjoy some juicy, succulent baby back ribs.

"Then FBI and military goons showed up out of thin air and basically kidnapped me and brought me here. But why? If what you say is true, I don't know how I can help. I'm a history professor who teaches and writes history books. I'm not a scientist, nor am I in the military."

Before Thomas could answer, a scowling, corpulent brigadier general stepped forward. I immediately felt an uneasiness about him. His breath smelled like burnt ass and popcorn and there was something...off about his vibe.

"Dr. Mazique, my name is General McGovern," he said, the medals on his military jacket shining brightly. "You were brought here because 10 years ago you wrote something called *Return to Nubia*."

It took me a second to remember the paper, though a few moments later the recollection seemed to come back in a sudden rush. When it did, I became more confused.

"Now I REALLY don't understand why I'm here! That paper was written in jest—a what-if answer to a question—about time travel."

McGovern huffed, "It was MORE than jest. You penned that paper with a couple of other so-called Black intellectuals; correct?"

So-called Black intellectuals? What in the hell? *Yeah, the general can get hit in his throat, too.*

I corrected McGovern. "I don't think any of us were 'so-called', General. We ARE intellectuals. That's why I'm called Dr. Mazique. The paper to which you're referring was based on a question rooted in fantasy: If Black people in America could go back in time to make things more equitable in the present, what period should they visit and what actions should they take?"

"And just what was YOUR response?"

I didn't particularly like his tone of voice. For some reason he appeared angry. This led me to give him the skinny—raw, and unfiltered—with no chaser.

"I wrote someone should go back in time and kill both John Wilks Booth and Andrew Johnson by removing their gonads and inserting them down their throats."

The general paused. Of course, he already knew what I had written. He just wanted to see if I had the balls to say it out loud.

In a reprimanding tone, he remarked, "You couldn't have left directions to just kill them? You had to be graphic by giving instructions to cut off their testicles and shove them into their mouths?"

Not knowing what McGovern's problem was, I smirked and responded, "You know Black people, we ALWAYS have to be extra. Besides, it's not like the two don't deserve it. While I'm not totally in love with Lincoln, I DO give him his respect because he was a president. I don't care about your feelings; don't EVER touch a president of the United States.

"And as far as Johnson is concerned, that racist, rapacious rat bastard deserves MORE than having his testicles removed."

I could tell McGovern didn't like that response, but instead of voicing his displeasure he instead said, "Some of your other...intellectual colleagues wrote differently. Why didn't you agree with them?"

"The question posed in the exercise specifically referenced Black Americans, not Black people worldwide from the diaspora. The solution for many was simply to go back before the advent of the slave trade and fire upon any European ship docking on African shores. This plan of action sounds simple and practical.

"It wouldn't be too hard to implement. There are historical logs. Dates. Times. Yet I felt the approach impractical and stupid."

"Why?"

"Assuming one could only take back so many people and modern weaponry at one time, there would be no way any single group could continuously keep the Europeans at bay. Keep in mind, there were limitations attached to this hypothetical question. The biggest was a person or group would only have one shot at, or be able to make one trip to the past.

"This is one of the reasons I didn't like the *Attack Africa* scheme. There was no way to replenish supplies. Eventually the ammunition, food, and other resources would run out. Besides, do you realize how many Africans were taken from the motherland? How many ships came to Africa?"

The general uttered, deadpan, "No, I do not. I don't get much into the CRT crap."

Figures. "Another thing. Even if you COULD prevent all of the slave ships from coming to Africa, that would mean Blacks never come to America—at least not in chains—and things would be different than they are now. For this reason, my paper focused on a period of time when African Americans were already in the United States and firmly entrenched, but I SPECIFICALLY picked the late Civil War era for precision.

"It reduced the number of people and weaponry needed to succeed. Only two men would have needed to be taken out, not a myriad of ships. If Booth were killed, Lincoln would have never been assassinated and his full plan of reconstruction would have been realized. Likewise, if Johnson were not around, there would have been a different vice-president—hopefully, one not as overtly and inwardly racist as Johnson.

"While Lincoln was far from the great messiah that Black people history books make him out to be, my theory was that if someone from the future showed him pictures of Barrack Obama and told him that eventually America would one day have a Black President, his resolve would grow infinitely larger. If Lincoln had never been assassinated and was therefore able to reinforce his efforts on reconstruction in the South—at least until the beginning of the 20th century—it would have made a huge difference.

"That extra push would have ensured more Black equality and equity in the present. I also wrote that I believed the ripple effect from Booth's and Johnson's deaths would have ensured the *Hayes/Tilden Compromise*, and *Plessy versus Ferguson* would have never materialized."

McGovern scowled. "As I said, I'm not really into history or ANY of that CRT crap. All I care about are a couple of rogue agents, and I need your help in retrieving them."

You really are one rude bastard.

"Okay. Maybe YOU don't understand ME? I still don't know why I'm here! Yes, I wrote a paper. It was theoretical. So what? Why am I...?"

"Because one of the rogue agents who entered the timestream," McGovern interrupted, shoving a picture into my hands in the process, "the man in charge of the OTHER rogue agents who followed, is a former student of yours. He's become a radicalized Black nationalist."

Upon hearing the deeper implication, my interest piqued tenfold. It no longer mattered whether I believed what anyone was saying. Glancing down at the picture, my eyes spied a familiar face.

The general continued. "His name is Major Darryl Lewis, and we believe he is attempting to use YOUR blueprint in *Return to Nubia* to alter the past."

That last statement made me want to double over and puke out my guts. It also left me short-winded and dazed. For once in my life, I had no witty retort or snappy comeback. The only thing I can remember thinking at that moment in time was, *WTF?!*

Chapter Two
trouble man

I figured Captain Lewis would seek me out after my lecture. I had, after all, gone hard in the paint in class and he often desired an audience with me after a provocative session. The subject matter and things covered in *The History of the Black Woman in America: Slavery to Present* often produced odd reactions.

His face today in the lecture hall amongst the other students had been the most contorted, though this in and of itself was not unusual. Lewis often wore his feelings on his sleeve, something I guess he had never really learned to control despite his maturity and age.

Attentive and always asking questions, I found him amiable. With a grin always on his face and a pep always in his step, he possessed the thirst for knowledge I wished all of my younger, traditional students had. All I knew about him was that he was on indefinite military furlough, about 10 years my junior, and possessed a very acute mind.

While some of his views were on the extreme side, I took them in stride. Lewis was a very passionate man and quite driven. He often rattled off his military accomplishments and informed me he was rather young to have made the rank of captain. Whatever.

I enjoyed our infrequent but heated debates and had been giddily anticipating the next. I found him to be more than my student: He was my intellectual equal and then some. Honestly, I don't know why he took the class. Perhaps officers in the military needed a certain amount of annual college credit.

"You had all of my attention today as usual," Captain Lewis said, coming up to me, cheesing from ear to ear.

I responded, "Well, I do like a captive audience. Are you ready to pick up on our debate where we left off the last time?"

"Yes, but I want a change of venue. Do you have time to go grab a coffee somewhere?"

Why not? I was through with classes for the day and couldn't resist the challenge. A good debate to me was like chess. It was a strategy that prepared a person for life. Win or lose, I always learned something new. I was already fired up from class and ready to argue.

"You're on," I told him. Fifteen minutes later, we were at a local Starbucks knee-deep in coffee.

After we had gotten comfortable, I asked, "You want me to go first or do you want to draw first blood?"

Captain Lewis appeared contemplative. "I really brought you here to talk about something else."

My curiosity piqued. A different topic over which to debate? Scrumptious! "What are we to quibble over this time?"

"Well...it's not so much a quibble as it is a discussion. You see, I have an assignment for the military I have to complete, one on unusual situations." There was a strategic pause.

I downed a throat full of coffee. "Okay. Go ahead."

"I know you don't like to talk much about it because you said it was just a silly paper born from the debauchery of Jägermeister and Fireball, but I would like to use your scenario from *Return to Nubia* for my assignment."

Oh, no! Not that damn paper again!

"Captain Lewis. When we first met, you asked me a million questions about that asinine paper. If I remember correctly, you initially sought me out and took one of my classes because of it. I'm sorry, I don't know what else I can add. Besides, I thought you said you were more or less done with the military?"

"Well, because of my...specialty, I probably will never fully be done with the military or they with me."

"And what is it you do for them?" I asked, thinking he would slip up and finally say. In the past, he had been evasive, always taking information but giving very little.

"Not much," Captain Lewis replied humbly, still

not directly answering the question, "just a little data and information mining. And that's the thing with the tech field, the military always throws these crazy scenarios at you so you'll stay sharp. For this assignment, there is no right or wrong answer, just the details and thoroughness of the plan. Another thing, it has to be an unusual situation with a very unconventional response."

"So, you're saying the question posed in *Return to Nubia* and the circumstances surrounding it fit the criteria of your class assignment for the military?"

"Precisely."

"Okay, but what else can I tell you that I haven't already said?"

Captain Lewis was assertive with his statement. "Well, so far I've mostly only asked you questions related to time travel."

"Yes, questions I told you I'm not qualified to answer, only theorize on. After all, I'm not a scientist. But you've also asked a lot of questions about key historical figures—mostly White—and what I think the ripple effects would be if they disappeared from history."

Captain Lewis began cheesing again. "What I need for this assignment," he said, "is something a little different."

"Go on."

"I need to plan the whole thing out, and I mean just that: Plan it out as though time travel is possible and John Wilks Booth and Andrew Johnson are the actual mission targets. Assuming an arrival destination and time in the past could be arranged, where would you send a team?

"How many would you send? What would they wear? What would they take back with them? What would be the exact year and date? Basically, I want you to tell me everything a group would need to carry this out."

Damn, I thought. *For that, I'm gonna need a hell of a lot more than coffee! Maybe another combination of Jägermeister and Fireball?*

I downed a large portion of java and said, "Okay, what the hell? I was ready for a good argument, but I guess I can argue a different way through history."

I looked at Captain Lewis, who seemed on the edge of anticipation.

"How thorough do you want me to be and how much time do you have on your hands?" I asked.

At the time, I didn't pay much attention to his response.

"I want you to be as thorough as possible," he gleefully stated. "And regarding how much time I have on my hands right now: Until death and taxes are no more. THAT'S how much time I have to listen to what you have to say."

I laughed. "Well, then, if that is the case, let us get started."

****

"Since I'm partially already in bed with you," I remarked, sitting in a comfortable chair in an underground bunker at Area 51, "can I ask how long the military has been messing around with the timestream?"

Thomas was happy to answer. With people like McGovern around, he probably didn't get to speak much.

"The military has been working on it for decades but only developed a working model seven years ago. Even then, all we could do is send inanimate objects through. We've just now built a working prototype that opens a portal humans can enter."

I began doing the math in my head, and the realization made me extremely angry. I hated to be bent over without any lubrication. Lewis had allowed my ego to play me. His whole presence in my classes had been a ruse to gather information for a plan so nefarious I shuddered to think what would happen if successful.

Oh, hell, what do I mean, I shuddered to think? I KNOW what will happen! I'm the dumbass who helped him plan it in the first place! Yet how was I to know what I was planning was real? I mean, it's not like anyone knew time travel was possible. Wait a minute...

22

"Why would the military even be mucking with the timestream anyway?" I asked.

Before anyone could answer, I continued, "It wouldn't make much sense they'd be interested in changing the past. They wouldn't know what would happen and there would be no value in retrieving weaponry to which they already had access.

"On the other hand, if the military went into the future, they wouldn't have to worry about disrupting the present but could stumble upon advanced weaponry and bring it back..."

McGovern cut in, "None of that is your concern. What IS your concern, what is OUR concern, is if you will be a part of the mission."

I wanted to agree if only to go back in time to kill one of McGovern's ancestors so he would never be born. The bigger issue, though, was that I had helped Captain, rather, Major Lewis along with his scheme. I was partially responsible, despite my ignorance. This meant I couldn't simply be a bump on a log and ignore my involvement.

Besides, I was a historian. What person in my situation wouldn't jump at the chance to go back in time, regardless of the risks? Forget prime sources, I could experience the past firsthand! No one could pass up that chance, least of all me.

"I'm in," I finally said after a long wait, "but only if you tell me what Major Lewis' job in the military was."

One of McGovern's eyebrows edged slightly higher than the other. I knew he wondered why I had made the request, but he didn't inquire.

"Understand that even though you're agreeing to go on this mission and you know about time travel, much of this we still can't discuss with you. And you're going to need to sign some forms right after we finish here."

"Yes. The military and their NDAs. I know all about the Kanye West-Kim Kardashian formalities."

"Good. Back to Major Lewis. Let's just say he has had several jobs with the United States military. He speaks five languages, has four degrees, one Ph.D., and is more or less trained to infiltrate and provide military reconnaissance from behind enemy lines.

"He knows military strategy in and out and how to sow the seeds of resentment amongst the populace of an unstable government in order to overthrow it. And even though he may not LOOK the part, don't let his humble façade fool you. Major Lewis can probably kill you 10 different ways simply with a writing pen."

McGovern should have also thrown in the words "calculating" and "patient". Lewis had been planning this for quite a long time. However, the only word standing out in my mind had been "reconnaissance".

Lewis had done this and I had willingly provided it.

"Now, before you sign any papers," McGovern uttered, glaring at me, "it's MY turn to pose a question to you."

WTF? Oh, this should be special!

"Go right ahead."

"Do you stand for the flag?"

I sense throat action!

Incredulously, I replied, "What did you ask me?"

McGovern reiterated what he had said with an inflected voice. "Do you stand for the flag?!"

"What does that question have to do with all the tea in China or in Britain or anything else relevant to what is occurring now?"

"It is VERY relevant to what is occurring now. Do you stand for the flag, or do you sit down in protest? Before we embark on this mission, I need to know."

I started to give him the full Dr. Mazique treatment but decided to only give him half since that's all he was worth.

"General, don't EVER question where I stand regarding America. The fact you even asked that question shows me where YOUR mentality stands. In my opinion, it's the very reason we have problems now. Do you want to know where I stand? If I rise for the flag?

"Yes, I do. Every damn time I hear the national anthem played. My people have begged to fight and have died in too many of this country's wars for me NOT to stand!"

Trying to be glib, McGovern retorted, "I didn't ask for a soliloquy, Dr. Mazique, just an answer."

"Well, I gave you one, anyway," I shot back. "Next time, don't insult my intelligence."

"Next time, simply answer. Don't be so sensitive."

And just like that, I had found a new nemesis, one I abhorred. I suppose it wasn't too early for me to begin wishing McGovern would end up missing in the timestream.

Chapter Three
team bonding

The pieces to a puzzle I never before knew existed today came together in my mind. A decade ago, my colleagues and I co-authored some supposedly theoretical papers on an impossible solution for what seemed like an asinine, frivolous question.

Though I received some acclaim and notoriety for the composition, I thought it was no big deal. I had published grander material with bigger accolades. *Return to Nubia*, however, made me a rising celebrity of the left, while putting a more recognizable target on my back for the conservative right at which to aim. Then four years after the paper's publication, I run into a shady, radicalized Black nationalist who pumps me for information to use *Return to Nubia* to equalize the playing field for African Americans.

Now, six years after I provided Major Lewis with all he needs, I make the reckless decision to accompany a team who is going after him. After signing the NDAs and being read everything but the riot act and having a cattle prod inserted into my rectum, I was ushered to another room, sat in front of a whole new panel of military bigwigs, and was given rules to follow. Most pertained to the timestream. The basic idea was not to contaminate it. Doing so could and would alter the past.

To be fair, what these idiots didn't understand was that any intrusion from the present was ALREADY a contamination. Time travel is perplexing and raises a lot of questions, but much of it is related to the butterfly effect and is a part of chaos theory. Yeah, I know, it all sounds like a bunch of bovine defecation, but follow me and I will try to make the smell more palatable.

To the naked eye, the flapping of a butterfly's wings means nothing, but each beat invisibly reverberates throughout the world. They set up conditions in a deterministic, non-linear environment. These reverberations pull and push people together to create history. Disturbing or altering the conditions comes with severe consequences. People who were supposed to cross paths might not ever meet and events that were supposed to take place might not ever occur. The movie *Back to the Future* is a perfect example.

Marty McFly, played by Michael J. Fox, goes back in time, with the help of an eccentric scientist, in style via a DeLorean car. Unfortunately, in doing so he inadvertently messes up the destinies of his father George and his mother Lorraine. She is the same age as Marty when he arrives in the past. Because he is different from the other boys, she becomes infatuated when she meets him. Lorraine rejects George, barely noticing he exists. Yet had Marty never gone back in the past, Lorraine would have become fixated on George as she did in the original timeline.

Part of the comedy of the film was Marty's efforts to convince Lorraine that George, not he, was the right man for her. Marty was very fortunate. If he had not been successful in undoing the damage his trek had made—interrupting the original reverberations of the butterfly's wings—his parents would have never married because the initial conditions had changed. This would have erased him from existence.

In such a case, Marty wouldn't have simply died, he would have been expunged. I wondered...how many reverberations would this mission interrupt? Moreover, how many had Major Lewis ALREADY interrupted? So far, there had been no noticeable historic deviations, but it was only a matter of time, no pun intended, before there would be.

This is one of the reasons why General McGovern already had a strike team assembled and ready to go through the portal. They had simply been waiting on me. They needed an advisor, someone who knew the social and political mores of the time.

There would only be five in the group, which I believed was a good thing. Even still, I wished the force could have been smaller. Fewer people meant less intrusion on the past, but there was no way to know what Major Lewis had already done or how many people would be needed to fix it.

The only thing I hated about the upcoming trip—
the one thing suddenly sprung on me at the last
minute—was the knowledge McGovern would be
coming along. Not only would he be coming along,
but he would also be leading the damn mission.
Besides vexing, I found this highly unusual.

McGovern seemed too high on the food chain to
be risked on such a dangerous mission. I had
watched enough *Star Trek* to know officers above a
certain rank are prohibited from doing so because
their leadership status makes them a high-priority
target. Even so, Captain Kirk would always ignore
this rule and lead the ship's away missions, though
the differences between Kirk and McGovern were
stark. Besides being of lesser rank, Kirk was
charismatic, while McGovern had all the charm of a
doorknob. I also got the feeling McGovern was
going along to keep a close eye on me.

Whenever we had been alone, he had diligently
used the time to pepper me with questions about
Major Lewis: What did I know? What did he ask
me? What did I tell him? Blah, blah, blah. Don't get
me wrong, part of me understood his hammering. I
was, after all, the source of inspiration for Lewis's
current shenanigans. Still, it was the manner of
McGovern's questions, as if somehow, I was in on
the whole thing, that got me.

Since I didn't trust him as far as I could spit, I

didn't tell him anything beyond the basics and certainly not the avid details I had given away to Major Lewis at Starbucks that day after class.

I wanted to tell the damn idiot no SANE man—regardless of his hatred for Whites or his love for Blacks—would EVER aid him. Mucking with the timestream for one race mucked the timestream for ALL races.

Who would risk their parents or ancestors never meeting and never being born? In many respects, helping Major Lewis was WORSE than suicide. While I wasn't quite fond of death, I was terrified of being wiped from existence. Having never been born seems so...gross. I didn't meet the rest of the team until about an hour before going through the portal. It was comprised of two men—one Chinese American and one Hispanic American—and one African American female.

All were around the same ages, either in their late 30s or early 40s, and all looked ready to be able to kick butt and take names. However, when I saw them, my suspicions about McGovern became even more heightened. There was something I didn't like about us going into the past, in the era to which we were traveling, with him being the sole White person. McGovern brought them all in at the same time to meet me, pointing and giving me the skinny on each.

"Dr. Mazique, this is Second Lieutenant Christian

Nguyen," he said, motioning over to the Chinese American. "His specialties are weapons and reconnaissance."

Tall and lean, Nguyen looked over at me and gave a silent nod.

"Next, is Second Lieutenant Tony Porras. His specialties are hand-to-hand combat and reconnaissance."

Short and stocky, Porras glanced up and spoke as if I were annoying him.

"Hello," he gruffly remarked.

I politely replied, "Nice to meet you." Inwardly I laughed to myself. *You're probably pissed off McGovern's coming along, too, huh?*

"Last, but not least," he said with a sly grin on his face, "is First Lieutenant Edith Reese. Her specialty is communications. She can speak 10 different languages, most notably several of the Indian dialects of the Old West. She's also a designated marksman and...is somewhat more familiar with Major Lewis than the rest of us."

I wasn't quite sure what McGovern's last statement meant, but I did notice how Reese reacted. Her right arm jerked slightly, as though a doctor had suddenly injected a needle. The general's words had stung. Another thing to which I paid attention was the inflection and tone of his words. The statement was a personal attack. To her credit, I could tell Reese hid her feelings well. Despite the arm flinches, she had remained stone-faced.

Also, unlike the other two, I could tell there was a difference with Reese. Light-skinned, medium height, and attractive, she didn't appear the type for this kind of mission. Her vibe was the antithesis of what this mission seemed to call for; hers was more independent, less compliant, and rebellious.

Just as Major Lewis had been in my classes, she seemed out of place in the current environment. Reese turned and hesitated for a second, looking me over. She nodded her head once her eyes locked onto mine. For some odd reason, I sensed she trusted me more than she did McGovern.

After the general had finished introducing the team to me, he attempted to introduce me to the team by revealing my background. This was his effort at mental manipulation. I was supposed to be overwhelmed and ashamed of the intrusion. I wasn't, but his effort still pissed me off to the full height of pisstivity itself. Grabbing a nearby manilla folder, McGovern read my whole life history.

"Dr. Mazique," he innocently unwound, "born George Bernard Mazique, March 1st, 1970, to Dr. Sebastian Mazique, Ph. D., and Attorney Dana Mazique."

He paused strategically and looked back at me. "It's so nice to see someone like you was raised in a nice, middle-class, educated environment because, regrettably, so many of you aren't."

There was another strategic pause before McGovern continued.

"Let's see…. Unfortunately, tragedy struck your family at a young age. When you were 11, your father died in a car accident. I see your accompanying rage later made you pretty good with your fists. You began to get suspended at school. There is even a notation here you knocked out your high school gym teacher and had to finish your senior year at an alternative school?"

He stopped and stared at me, waiting for me to react with rage. Instead, I reacted with rhetoric.

"I'm kind of sensitive about people talking about my life," I said, not giving him a chance to continue, "especially when I'm in the room. If you don't mind, I'll control my narrative?"

With the manilla folder still wide open, McGovern made a sweeping gesture with one of his hands. "Go right ahead."

"As you read out loud, I became good with my hands. So good I began to use them in the ring and won the city's Golden Glove contest by the time I was 18 years old. Unfortunately, as fate would have it, my mother died not long after from cancer. It seems a young tyke like me couldn't catch a break. I was destinated to be alone. And it's probably one of the reasons I've never wed. My work and my writing consume me.

"Anyway, I'm sure you have it all in your folder there somewhere that my mother's dying wish was for me to become an academician, not a brute. So, despite my proclivities for using my hands, and despite my anger issues, I began to hone my mind the same way I had my physicality.

"History had always fascinated me, so that's where I threw in my lot. The rest is, as they say, history. I've studied under Drs. Molefi Asante, Obidike Kamau, Cornell West, AND Henry Louis Gates, Jr. I have two Ph. Ds.—in political science and history—with concentrations in military strategies of generals of color and African American history.

"I'm neither as young as most of you, nor do I do this for a living, but I promise not to be much of a burden on this mission. I stay active in the gym and know how to shoot a gun, although I'm no Nat Love."

"Who?" McGovern asked, not familiar with the name. I knew he wouldn't be. That's why I used it.

"Nat Love," Porras responded for me, still acting as though he were being bothered. "He was a Black cowboy."

Nguyen chimed, "And how do YOU know that?"

Porras rebuked him. "Because I read, dummy!"

This presented the perfect opportunity to hit back at McGovern. I glared at him.

"Good thing you do, Porras. Some people consider knowledge like that CRT crap."

Without circling back to me, McGovern suddenly barked, "That's enough with the introductions. Be dressed and ready to go within the hour. Meet back at the portal, locked and loaded, at 0500."

Walking away, McGovern mean-mugged me and I returned the favor.

Porras and Nguyen scrambled out together. As they did, I could hear Nguyen ask Porras, "They REALLY had Black cowboys?"

I waited and glanced at Reese, who glanced back at me. When she finally moved to make her way out of the room, I motioned for her to stop.

Not really knowing what to say or how to begin, I uttered, "I'm sorry, I know you don't know me from a hill of beans, but before you go...do you mind telling me what McGovern meant when he said you were more familiar with Major Lewis than any of us?"

At first, I didn't know if she was going to give me an answer. Her response wasn't immediate. She locked onto my eyes, once again gazing intently, analyzing for trust. Reese saw something worthy in them.

At long last, before exiting, she tepidly stated with no emotion, "Major Lewis is my fiancé."

After hearing this, I couldn't help, but think, *now, ain't THAT some shit!*

Chapter Four
the south shall rise again

I was impressed with the clothing picked out for the mission. Though what had been gathered had been thrown together haphazardly, we were clothed appropriately for the era. If we didn't blend in as a group, it wouldn't be because we didn't look like the others. It would be because we didn't ACT like the others, but that's where I came in as an advisor: To steer the group in the right direction when it came to interacting with the public.

The only problem with this is the period to which we were going. North or the South, there weren't many Black men in America advising White men in any manner. When interacting in public with the group—especially with McGovern—I would have to remain especially vigilant in maintaining humility.

While there were outspoken Black men of the day, like David Walker or Frederick Douglass, they were not plentiful. Nor did they have to be overly concerned about drawing attention to themselves and upsetting the timeline any more than it already had been. I did.

The one thing about which I was consulted before we departed involved guns. More specifically, I was asked what I thought about bringing modern weaponry and ammunition along.

———

There was also talk of laptops that could operate with solar power.

I was against taking back anything not from the original period. Something could happen and if anyone in the past discovered future technology or weaponry, it would only prove disastrous to the timestream. Several scientists had already told the bigwigs this.

The military compromised by providing the team with small semi-automatic handguns and ammunition tucked secretly away in rucksacks on the soldiers' backs. McGovern, being the sole White male out of the group, had the only visible weapon, which rested snugly in a holster on his hip. It was an era-appropriate, vintage, six-shot Remington model 1858 pistol.

Unfortunately, being a civilian, I was the only one without any type of weapon, but in a way I was grateful. Having access to a gun drew me closer to my past, to the violent tendencies I had long ago given up after my mother's death. I was now a historian, not a warrior or a soldier. Besides, I had my fists and I knew how to use them far better than any pistol I would ever hold.

After the team had assembled in front of the time portal, the rest of the staff—about 15 scientists and military personnel—came to see us off. Thomas waved his hands to get everyone's attention. He pulled out what appeared to be five sleek, slick-designed ebony watches.

He handed one to everyone on the team, walking over to each individually and showing us how to wrap it around our wrist. As it locked into place, it made a high-pitched chiming sound. When he was done, he backed up a couple of feet and held up his right arm. When his sleeve fell, everyone could see he had a mechanism attached to him as well.

"As you've probably surmised by now, this is not a watch," he said. "It is a chronal spatial adjustor."

Nguyen asked, "A what?"

"A chronal spatial adjustor," Thomas restated. "It serves two purposes. The first is that it will return you here, to your original timeline." He showed everyone what button to push, and how long to hold it, whenever we chose to return.

"The second purpose of this device," he continued, "is perhaps the most important." Thomas sighed and took his time as if to adjust his thoughts.

"If this team is unsuccessful in apprehending Major Lewis and bringing him back, the change to the timeline will reverberate and alter things completely.

"If that happens, no one knows who might be erased or changed. Even if you are in the past, if the present timestream is affected it could prove fatal to you. This device will prevent that from happening."

"Even if the original timestream is affected?" I questioned.

"Yes."

"So, this keeps us alive by not allowing the chronal anomaly from sweeping us into the altered reality? An altered reality where we might not exist?"

"Precisely," Thomas answered. "It will keep the team alive and able to return to fix whatever timestream changes have been made without anyone having to worry about being expunged from the universe."

I still needed some additional information. "But what about everyone here? If changes to the past are made, if we return and everyone here has been erased..."

"Don't worry about that," Thomas uttered, motioning to the personnel to raise their arms.

"Everyone here has on a chronal spatial adjustor. Believe me, these things weren't cheap to make, but the military realizes the importance of keeping people around who can operate the machinery." He paused for a second to look at everyone.

"Any more questions?"

There was a long silence before Porras finally yelled, "Man, let's get this shindig on the road!"

McGovern seconded with, "My sentiments exactly, Lieutenant."

Lost in all of the hoopla of the moment, though, was one very crucial question, but not because I had forgotten to ask it. In agreeing to go back in time to apprehend Major Lewis, I had assumed he had stuck to the original plan the two of us had drawn up that day at Starbucks. Because of this, there was no need for me to inquire about the year to which he had returned or where he was headed. I already knew...or, at least, I assumed I did.

Reese raised her hand. "One last question. Are we just shooting blanks in the past, or do we have a specific year and location for Major Lewis?'

"No," Thomas added, as though it were no big deal, "we know where he is and McGovern has the coordinates. Major Lewis went back in time to 1862, somewhere in Tennessee. We can accurately pinpoint his location up to five to eight miles from where he arrived. It was somewhere in Greene County."

Greene County?! Greene County?! WTF? My eyes grew bigger than the federal deficit. The bewilderment must have shown on my face, because McGovern noticed it.

"What's wrong, Dr. Mazique?"

I didn't try to hide my anger.

"You KNEW we were going back in time to a slave

state a year after the Civil War started and you didn't think to tell anyone?"

Nguyen and Porras exchanged glances with each other.

"No," he condescendingly replied. "This is a military mission back into time. The year and location don't matter."

"Maybe not to YOU it doesn't! YOUR people weren't the ones chopping the cotton and getting lynched!"

"Dr. Mazique, *Return to Nubia* was YOUR plan, remember? To go back in time and make things all nice and cozy for Black people? You knew the approximate period. Where did you THINK we were headed?"

"To Washington D.C., a couple of weeks before Lincoln was assassinated," I told him.

"And why would you think that?"

It's what Major Lewis and I agreed.

"Because it's what I would have done. Logistically it makes the most sense. The war was at its end. Johnson would have been around Lincoln at some point, with Booth to later follow. I would simply set up shop, lay low, and let them come to me."

McGovern snapped, "Well, evidently THAT didn't happen. The chronal energy and data left in the timestream portal suggest otherwise."

He paused before asking, "Is this a problem?"

For some reason, right at that moment, I was compelled to look over at Reese, who was glancing at me at the same time. We seemed to be falling into the habit of talking to one another through facial expressions. For whatever reason, hers told me she needed my help to complete the mission. They also continued to tell me she trusted McGovern even less than I did. For these reasons, I decided not to challenge the general any further.

You witless, wannabe, White, imitation Colin Powell!

"No, it's not a problem," I finally answered. "But in the future, I would appreciate it if you were not so secretive with information. While you may not think it makes a difference, it does. If I'm supposed to advise, let me in on things so I can make a proper assessment."

McGovern cracked a sadistic grin. "Kiss my ass" was written all over it.

Issuing an obviously half-empty apology, he sardonically remarked, "I'm sorry for the oversight, Dr. Mazique. In the future, I will endeavor to do better. Now, may we please be on our way?"

Out of the pan and into the fire I go…

Chapter Five
back to the past

I would describe in detail what time travel feels like, but since I'm STILL attempting to pry open my butt cheeks, I will spare you of all the gory details. Let's just say it felt as though my brain was pregnant and about to give birth. The sensory overload was painful, sudden, and debilitating. Once on the other side, it took a while to get my bearings, though I'm glad to say I was not alone. Everyone was more or less discombobulated.

Thankfully, it was a little after midnight when we made it through the portal. The cover of darkness and the rolling forests of Greene County, Tennessee, concealed our presence as we scrambled to place ourselves amongst the tall, untamed oak and white pine trees. I knew we were no longer in the present, but it was a trip actually seeing 1862 at night up close and personal.

The only illumination was in the sky amongst the stars. Ground level, darkness consumed everything. Foolishly, I scanned the area. There was no lamppost or light to be seen amongst the mountains in the distance. Then I remembered. The lightbulb won't be invented until 17 years from now and electricity won't start to become commercially distributed until 1882. Plus, the country is at war.

Any type of illumination might draw the wrong type of attention. Because of this heightened uncertainty, we found a thick cluster of forest connecting to an open, wide field.

The group inserted itself deep into the woods, facing the field. If someone or another party approached, it would give us time to determine whether they were friend or foe. The team hadn't brought along much modern technology, but it did have several pairs of night vision binoculars.

Everyone would take turns, in shifts of two, standing watch on the edge of the forest leading to the field. Luckily, Lieutenant Reese and I were chosen for the second shift. I had long been wanting to grab some more alone time to ask questions about Major Lewis and what else she might know. We would be far enough away from the group to have a discreet conversation.

Reese had taken out her sidearm from her rucksack. The pistol lay across one of her legs as she sat on the ground, her back against a tree. With the binoculars pressing against her face, she scanned the field with diligence for any sign of trouble. Despite my lack of a weapon, I was unfettered by confidence. Reese's demeanor and diligence told me she was more than capable of putting a well-aimed shot into someone's gluteus maximus.

Every few seconds I would catch her glancing up

at me, reading my facial expressions. I felt as though she wanted to say something but didn't know how to start the conversation. Well, I am a no-nonsense type of man and she seemed to be a no-nonsense type of woman. Perhaps all it took was for one of us to open our mouth.

"Do you mind if I ask you a few questions about Major Lewis?" I finally asked. I didn't know if she had heard me. Reese didn't respond until a few seconds later. She placed the binoculars down on her lap.

"Yes, I DO mind," she softly responded, "but I also know your questions are necessary, if for no other reason than for you to understand what is really going on."

What did she mean by that?

"Did you know Major Lewis was going to do this? Go back in time to change the past?"

Reese put the binoculars to her face, waiting a few moments before answering, "No." Then I saw her arm twitch. This was understandable. I had felt the sadness in her voice.

"So that means…"

She yanked the binoculars from her face and interrupted me. "That he really didn't give a damn about me, because changing the timeline might erase me from existence?" Reese asked.

"Well, yes, my second question was going to be something along those lines."

She turned all the way around to stare behind us, checking to see if anyone was listening. Seeing the coast was clear, she reached into one of her pockets and removed something. Bringing it closer to my eyes, I saw it was another chronal spatial adjustor.

"I received this via courier about a day before the shit hit the fan. It was from Darryl...I mean Major Lewis. It didn't come with a note, just a little sticky explaining the gift as something very important for me to wear, a unique present symbolizing his love."

"So why didn't you put it on?"

"Because every woman should know their man and I DEFINITELY knew my fiancé. I was getting a vibe something was amiss. Besides, the sticky also came with a warning to wear the bracelet underneath a long-sleeved shirt or to keep it in my pocket. That seemed kind of shady to me. Normally when Major Lewis would give me a gift, he wanted me to show it off to the world. Hell, normally I wanted to show it off to the world.

"I was glad I didn't put it on, though. The Secret Service and military kicked in my door the next day, searched the entire place from head to toe, and then questioned me for hours on end."

I had to ask. "So where did you hide the thing, then? If they didn't find it?"

Reese's smirk was so wide, I could see it clearly through the darkness of the night.

"There are some things a man should NEVER ask

a woman," she remarked.

"Oookay," I let out with slight embarrassment.

Time to switch gears.

"Well, I know it's no way to look at it, but at least you know Major Lewis really loves you. Sending the bracelet means he thought of you. He planned ahead to make sure you wouldn't accidently be expunged."

Reese suddenly went silent. Grabbing the binoculars once more, she stared through its lenses in both directions relative to our position, behind and in front. After a while had passed, she appeared more contemplative. The binoculars returned to her lap.

"Dr. Mazique, this whole thing is bigger than you know. It's bigger than I know. McGovern was right when he told you Major Lewis performed a lot of different tasks for the military. He was also investigating McGovern."

My left eyebrow raised. "Does McGovern know this?"

"No, at least I don't BELIEVE so."

"Do you know WHY Major Lewis was investigating him?"

"No," Reese huffed, "but he had been looking into him and others for about seven years. That's why he was originally transferred into the military's Chronal Spatial department. With his background, it was the perfect cover. Not surprisingly, Major Lewis and McGovern never got along."

I couldn't help being sarcastic. "Let me guess. Because McGovern has such a rosy personality?"

"Yeah, something like that," she replied wickedly. "All I know is that when Major Lewis became a part of McGovern's unit, his personality began to change."

"What do you mean?"

"Despite Major Lewis and I only being together for three years, we had been close friends for a little over 10 years. We had ALWAYS been attracted to one another but thought our personalities too strong for a relationship to ever last. We both don't take any... Well, you know what I'm trying to say. Thing is, with time we got older and matured enough to make things between us work out.

"Major Lewis has always been dedicated to the Black community and maintained an interest in helping the poor and disfranchised. But when he transferred into that military unit, he started to become...angry all of the time."

"Angry about what?"

"About White people. The state of the United States. Take your pick. It could have been the public backlash against Collin Kaepernick or the unjust killings of people like Breonna Taylor, George Floyd, or Eric Garner."

50

"So," I asked, trying to better understand, "Major Lewis was angry about the rising racism in the United States? Black people getting killed by the White police?"

"It wasn't just that," Reese clarified. "He had always struggled with his rage, controlling himself, when it came to some people's intolerance of others. No, this anger was new and different. It was almost as if being around McGovern and his group highlighted his fears. He became extremely paranoid. He started ranting about how White people were going to eventually wipe Blacks from existence. I thought he was crazy and suggested he see a shrink. But, like I said earlier, I KNOW my man and I knew he wasn't crazy. Just slightly off."

"Then you found out about the time machine," I said.

"Yes, and now things are beginning to make a little more sense. But everything else revolves around McGovern. He thinks he's watching me, but I'm the one watching HIS ass."

I hope she meant that figuratively, because looking at his ass literally makes me want to throw up!

"One other thing you should know," Reese added, "Nguyen, Porras, and I were briefed before you arrived. Major Lewis rigged the portal, which they are STILL attempting to fix."

"What do you mean, he rigged the portal? It seemed to be working to me. We came out okay, even though I'm still walking kind of funny."

Reese shook her head. "Did you ever wonder why the military didn't simply jump right back to the exact moment BEFORE Major Lewis went into the timestream to apprehend him? If that had been the case, they wouldn't have needed you and everything could have been swept under the rug."

"Well, that HAD occurred to me, but I thought maybe it was because it was prohibited by rules tied to the timestream."

"No. It's because he rigged it to blow if it were used to go to any era but this period. The military eventually will fix whatever he did, but they didn't have time to wait. They had to send a team back now, before any damage to the timestream could occur."

Major Lewis, you sneaky bastard.

"So Major Lewis forced the military to come back to the exact time he arrived? That means he KNOWS we're coming for him? This is a trap!"

"Precisely. But one of the reasons Major Lewis and I are together is because we think alike. It's exactly what I would have done, particularly if I were trying to capture a rat that's too fat and protected in the present."

It was at that moment a quote from Sir Walter Scott's **Marmion** came to mind. *Oh, what a tangled* *web we weave, when we first practice to deceive...*

Chapter Six
sunrise

General McGovern was the last to stand watch. Because the group was an odd number and everyone else had participated in a shift, he performed his alone. This was probably a good thing. Judging from Nguyen's and Porras' body language, he hadn't endeared himself to them, either.

Reese had explained that while they were a part of the Chronal Spatial department, they had only been recently assigned to McGovern. Having been yanked into this situation because of her ties to Major Lewis, she wasn't very familiar with them, either. Of course, Nguyen and Porras gave McGovern his respect because he was in charge.

Yet being in charge and being a leader were different things. Soldiers will do as they are told, but they will go to the depths of Hell to fight the devil himself if they are commanded by a leader. McGovern was no leader. He would be lucky if soldiers under his command were motivated enough to mount a proper defense against Buckwheat.

By 0500, the team began to ready itself to be on the move before the sun rose. I was the first to finish and walked to meet the general at the edge of the forest to ask what our next steps would be.

"Did you sleep well, Dr. Mazique?" he queried when I approached.

"As well as I could sleep on the ground without a pillow after going through a blender. Or at least that's what it felt like after going through the timestream."

He laughed. "If you think THAT was something, you should eat my wife's cooking!"

Someone married YOUR ass? May the Lord have mercy on their soul!

"Have you put together which direction we are going?"

"Actually, I was going to ask what YOU thought our first course of action should be," McGovern stated. "After all, you're the expert. And while you're at it, perhaps you can explain to me your hatred for Andrew Jackson."

"Andrew Johnson," I said, correcting him.

Flustered, he responded, "Andrew Jackson, Andrew Johnson, what's the difference?"

I had to school the general on history and presidents. "When it comes to the Andrews," I replied, transforming into professor mode, "it DOES make a difference. One has to make a distinction because both were presidents who were flaming racists."

McGovern cracked a smile. "I think you tend to believe EVERY president was racist."

"That's rich coming from someone who's White.

Your people weren't chattel slaves. Besides, it's not what I think of every president. It's what history tells me. Almost all of the early ones—George Washington and Thomas Jefferson included—owned slaves. How am I, as a Black man, SUPPOSED to view them? It definitely doesn't compel me to put a picture of either on my wall."

"So, what if they owned slaves? EVERYONE owned slaves back then! You can't take the moralities of the modern era and apply them to the past."

"That's the excuse commonly given, but I don't buy that either. If you read Washington or Jefferson's own words, they KNEW, morally, slavery was a sin, but they still had slaves. We know slavery is a sin now, and they knew it was a sin then too.

"Regarding Andrew Jackson, though, the barbarism was taken to another level. As a general before he became president, one of old Stonewall's nicknames was *The Great Indian Killer*. He is the one most responsible for the tragic deaths and genocide of the Native Americans who were forced to march along the **Trail of Tears**, which drove most into Arkansas and Oklahoma."

"And Andrew Johnson?" McGovern questioned, this time making sure he got the name correct.

I sighed. "Most people don't understand Andrew

Johnson was a Democrat, not a Republican. The reason he fell in with the Republicans was he was the only Democratic senator who did not give up his seat when the South succeeded from the Union. He never really embraced the Republican values of that era. It was only through a series of life's twists he later ended up becoming Abraham Lincoln's vice-president.

"By the time John Wilks Booth assassinated Lincoln, the Civil War was coming to an end. Lincoln had already laid out his plans for Reconstruction in the South. It leveled the playing field for Blacks and the poor. Reconstruction was the first time Black men were able to vote. It was also the first time Blacks began receiving a proper education.

"The result was a number of Blacks in Congress, people like Hiram Revels and Blanche K. Bruce. Johnson sought to tear Reconstruction down. He allowed many of the southern leaders who had led the Confederate army back into leadership positions. And what do you think was one of the first things those former Confederate leaders did? Especially after they had lost the war and their cash cow of slaves? They sought revenge against Black people and Johnson helped them obtain it. He enabled the Black codes which Southern White men erected to keep Blacks in their place.

"I could go on and on, but I won't. Regarding Johnson's overall abilities in the office, let's just say he was the first president to ever be impeached."

I was surprised the general had let me say all of that without interruption. Once I had finished, he asked. "So, you blame Johnson for Reconstruction's failure?"

"Reconstruction didn't fail, White America failed Reconstruction."

"Why? Because it didn't want to continue to pay exorbitantly for a social experiment?"

I paused, and not because McGovern had used a five-syllable word. I paused because his last statement proved he knew more about the subject than he had led me to believe. It was a classic argument many detractors of Reconstruction made.

"And why would you call Reconstruction a social experiment?"

"Educating ex-slaves? People who couldn't even read? Job training for people who had never held a job? Seems like wasted money, if you ask me."

"During Reconstruction, over 2,000 Black men held public office, all the way up to the Senate. And even after Reconstruction's demise and efforts to slow the education of Blacks down—with things like ***Plessy versus Ferguson*** in our way—our literacy rate STILL increased from 20% in 1870 to 70% by 1910.

"An exorbitant social experiment? No, more like a debt owed. Slaves weren't paid, so as far as I figure, Reconstruction was just America paying African Americans part of their due."

McGovern finally conceded. "Yes, I'm sure someone like you would see it like that. At any rate, maybe it's best to table this debate and go back to my original question. What do you think our course of action should be?"

"There are probably a couple of reasons Major Lewis came back to this period. For one, Greenville, Tennessee, is where Andrew Johnson lived. By 1862, the North had retaken most of Tennessee. Lincoln made Johnson the state's military governor. Johnson became vice-president in part as a reward for his loyal service to the Union and for national unity. My thinking is Major Lewis is now somewhere in Greenville waiting for Johnson to pass through. He will simply pick him off and move on to his next target."

"So, we should head toward Greenville?"

"Yes, but we have to be careful. For all intents and purposes, Tennessee will be a slave state until the end of the war."

Trying to be funny, McGovern retorted, "Seems like that's more a problem for YOU than for me, huh?"

I didn't waste my time giving him the stank eye.

He wasn't worth it. Instead, I simply stated, "It's settled, then. We head East toward Greenville."

Fifteen minutes later we started off marching through the woods. Eventually this led us to a well-traveled dirt road we assumed went into town. McGovern decided we should follow it. It would be faster than going through the forests and we couldn't avoid contact with the public forever. At some point, we would have to talk to others to gather clues as to Major Lewis' whereabouts.

After consulting with the rest of the group, we proceeded in a more cautious fashion along the dirt road. I made sure to keep a pair of binoculars in my hand. I wanted to see ahead of us; what might be coming our way, and how we might best mentally prepare for it. I was also attempting to put together a back story for our group. It was hindered due to its racial composition.

Reese and I were simple to explain. We were Black and the country was currently fighting a war over the status of our people. But what of Porras and Nguyen? In 1862, the armies of France and Mexico were fighting. There wouldn't be many Mexicans this far east in that time period.

Nguyen was a different story. By now there were a growing number of Chinese in America, but they were all on the other side of the continent, getting abused and helping to build the transcontinental railroad. I wagered most White men on this side had never seen someone who was Asian. If the situation had not been so dire, I would have snickered. It was easier promoting our group as the Village People than providing an era-appropriate, believable back story.

We had been making good time and were about two hours into our trek when I noticed some movement ahead. Motioning to the team to stop, I raised the binoculars and nervously peered a half mile up front. Taking my time before launching into a panic, I made sure my mind was not deceiving me. I could feel the team waiting with bated breath for some type of reaction.

Aware of this, I tried not to offer any. If I didn't panic, I believed the others wouldn't panic, either. I exhaled softly and brought the binoculars slowly down to the side of my body. I could feel Reese staring at the back of my head.

"Well?" she questioned rather aggressively. "What did you see?"

A part of me wanted to fly off the handle to see how she would react, but this was no time for games. She would have taken off my head and I wouldn't have blamed her. This encounter was going to be the real deal and mentally jarring.

Instead, I calmly replied, "There is a wagon with horses and White men carrying supplies, with a couple of slaves following closely behind. Some of the slaves are bound by chains attached to the wagon and some are not."

Looks of terror instantly overcame Nguyen's and Porras' faces. Reese was a little more direct.

Pulling out her sidearm, she exclaimed, "Oh, hell no! I DID not come back to the past to be ANYONE'S slave!" McGovern was quick to pull rank.

"Lieutenant, conceal your sidearm and control your emotions," he snarled. "Now! You WILL NOT do anything to put this mission in jeopardy. Do you understand me?"

Complying with his order, Reese begrudgingly said, "Yes, sir." Her arm began to twitch.

McGovern looked in my direction with a slightly concerned expression. "What do you think we should do?"

Shoot the White people, free the slaves, and then continue to kick rocks onto Greenville.

While I still hadn't thought of anything actually suitable, I usually did my best reflection when under pressure. This situation proved no different.

I suddenly had an epiphany. I knew what we had to do...what I had to do to make the mission succeed, although it was going to be extremely demeaning.

Yet I had to look at things from a historical context. What I was about to endure for only a few minutes, many of my ancestors had endured for a lifetime. Who was I to complain when we were attempting to save the world?

The needs of the many outweigh the needs of the few or the one.

"Take off your rucksack and give it to me," I told McGovern. He looked at me oddly.

"What?"

"Take off your rucksack and give it to me. We have to recognize in what time period we are and what we have to deal with. You are White, we are not, and this is a slave state. If we say we are freedmen, they might challenge us and it would complicate things. However, if we say we are your slaves, they won't even bat an eye."

McGovern looked at all of us and shook his head. "That might work for you and Reese, but how am I going to explain Nguyen and Porras?"

I looked down at the ground for a stick.

"Leave Nguyen and Porras to me," I uttered, finding a branch that was not too heavy or too big. I handed it to McGovern.

"Why did you give me this?" he asked, perplexed.

There was no time for a long explanation.

"Listen. Both of my parents were from Arkansas. Before they went to college and made it in their careers, their families were poor. Dirt poor. Both sides picked cotton and both sides lived through segregation and integration.

"Knowing some of what they had to endure, I have some idea of the mentality of the southern White men of this era. Just follow my lead and we will all be okay. If you have to hit me with the stick, make sure to hit me on my back and not on my head. It won't hurt as bad."

McGovern still appeared dumbfounded, as did the rest of the team, but he took off his rucksack and gave it to me. I made sure Reese concealed her firearm, and we continued to march toward the wagon and its caravan.

Before the oncoming group could get a good view of us, I arranged the team in a single-file line: McGovern in the front, me behind him with two rucksacks on my back, Reese behind me, Porras, and then Nguyen. The last thing I told the team before coming into earshot of the other group was both puzzling and vexing for them at the same time.

"You all are going to have to trust me on this, but I need you to play to racial stereotypes, no matter how distasteful it may be. You will get a better picture of what I'm talking about when I break into character."

Reese's face struggled to hold back her nervousness. Strategizing over the possibilities of what may occur from the coming encounter, I viewed her as our weakest link and it wasn't because she was fearful. With the exception of McGovern, I was sure we were ALL fearful.

No, First Lieutenant Reese was our weakest link because she was our most rebellious. History related that rebellion brought about adversity for slaves. I would have to pay special attention to her, though for the moment I tried not to look at her or her twitching arm.

When we came closer, our team saw the horror of what we were up against. There was a total of four White men. Two rode up front in the wagon, which was drawn by four horses, while the other two rode in the back with the supplies. In tow behind them were eight slaves, two without restraints and six with them.

While the unrestrained slaves appeared how I had more or less pictured they would, the chained slaves looked absolutely deleterious. Scantily clothed and badly beaten, they struggled through the pain of their scarred bodies to keep up with the wagon's pace.

I figured the unshackled slaves were owned by someone and already working in the fields. As such, they were already trained and knew not to buck their master. They didn't have to have chains on them. Of course, if such false freedom ever induced them to become froggy, all of the White men who were armed would lessen their resolve.

Contrary to popular opinion, the average plantation or family down South which engaged in slavocracy only had about four to five slaves. As such, plantations seen in movies like *Gone with the Wind* which was affluent enough to have house and field slaves, only represented the one percent owing 100 or more.

I figured whoever owned this caravan and its cargo, while not exactly rich, was not necessarily poor, either. If the person had enough money to buy six new adult slaves outright, he/she was worth a decent amount of change. I had advised McGovern to keep walking toward the wagon slowly and unsuspectingly.

At some point, one of the White men would address him. That is when the fun would begin. The man driving the wagon pulled on the reins of the horses when we were starting to pass to the right of their group.

He conversed with McGovern in a thick country drawl.

"Howdy. How yar doin'?"

Glancing over at the rest of us and then back at him, he queried, "I undastand the niggars and the two others walkin', mista, but why'n rn't ya ridin' a hose?"

I studied the man who seemed the oldest of the bunch. He had long gray hair that sat underneath a wide, straw, country hat. A pistol rested prominently on the side of his hip. Despite his speech being difficult to understand, I was familiar enough with country speech to comprehend what he had asked. Why wasn't McGovern riding on a horse instead of walking with his slaves?

I could see both of Reese's arms convulsing furiously, as if her body were going through withdrawals. I knew if I resented being called a nigger, she unequivocally abhorred it. To her credit, she didn't break character.

McGovern, though, hesitated. I could tell he was stuck like a deer in a headlight, not knowing what to say. This meant it came down to me to save the day. It would take my best Stepin Fetchit imitation.

"Why, sur," I began to say, "my masta's name is de Honirirble Judge McGovern from Lil' Rack, Arkunsaw. We wuz camped durn last nat, and a got dang black bear came and scurred the dang hos off!"

The White man never looked my way or addressed me. He continued to look at McGovern. This didn't upset me. I had expected it.

"Yar a judge?" he asked McGovern. "Whatca dooin' so fa from Lil' Rack?"

Catching on to my ruse, the general replied, "I have some business in Greenville to take care of."

He didn't try to fake a country accent or need to dumb down. Since I had painted him as a judge, he was expected to be educated and he wouldn't need to speak in a country dialect. His accent would betray him as a Northerner, but since they thought he possessed slaves, the men in the wagon would probably give him a pass.

He might not speak country, I contemplated about McGovern, *but he sure does speak asshole!*

"Whal, Judge McGovran, it's nas to meet ya. My nam is Jeb Coltrane. This heea on my rait is my sone, John. The yungin' in the back is my sone Cleophus. The otha in the back is my ovaseea, Mr. Johnson."

Out of the four, Mr. Johnson appeared to be the last one with whom I wanted to tangle. He was the only person in their group whose face was expressionless. With a wide black leather hat on his greying head and a long rifle in his hand, the only thing he appeared concerned with was maintaining order over the slaves. Paying no attention to the conversation at hand, he eyed all the Blacks, even the unrestrained, with evil contempt. I could see John and Cleophus looking oddly at Nguyen and Porras.

They jumped off the wagon and began making their way over. "Nice to meet all of you, Jeb. Do you mind telling me how far it is to Greenville?" McGovern asked.

"Nat too fur," Jeb told him. "If'n ya stay on thus rad, on foot, ya shad mak it thur by late afturnun."

By now, the two brothers were poking and prodding Nguyen, as if he were some animal at a petting zoo. Though I'm sure Nguyen wanted to knock the hell out of them, he did not react. Ironically, he had a very relaxed, comical expression across his face.

"Wat kinda damn slav is this? I ain't neva seent slavs that luk lak dese two!"

Once again, it was time for me to establish the narrative.

"Masta McGovern real smart," I interjected, putting on an Oscar-winning performance. "He real smart. Dat one rat dere is whatca call Chinese. He coam all de way from de Orient.

"He nat a slav, but masta McGovern wun him in a cad game and gonna sand him back West to woke on de railroad. De gonna sand all de money he mak back to masta. He speaks no Englash and is durmb as bracks."

As if on cue, Nguyen opened his mouth with a big wide grin and said in a heavy Asian accent that had not before been present, "Me speaka no English. Me speaka no English."

The two brothers turned to each other and began laughing hysterically. "Yep," Cleophus said, "he sho is durmb!"

I thought they would turn their attention to Porras. I was perfectly prepared to establish his backstory, but suddenly they were drawn to Reese and I realized my lack of foresight. She should have been the FIRST I thought about in this scenario. White male southern slave owners were notorious for their treatment of African American women.

Approximately 58% of Black female slaves, aged 15 - 30, were sexually assaulted during slavery. What made things particularly harrowing for them, though, is that it was not against the law to rape a slave. The ***State of Missouri versus Celia, a Slave*** clearly established slaves were property and slave owners could do whatever they wanted. Black female slaves could not even pick their own husbands. Most were told whom they would marry—for breeding purposes—and/or they had to get permission from the slave master.

With such intimate, draconian control of their lives, it is no wonder many White men thought it their right to rape their female slaves. Modern DNA from his offspring and historical records prove even the esteemed Thomas Jefferson either raped or had consensual sex—depending on the viewpoint—with Sally Hemings, his favorite slave and mistress.

Reese was an attractive woman. I hadn't thought about making her appear less so before we had departed through the portal. However, even if I HAD thought of this dilemma, how does someone make another appear aesthetically unpleasing? I didn't have a makeup artist who could instantly turn her into Shabba Ranks.

Please, don't snap, Reese! Please, don't snap!

The two brothers had moved close to Reese, one on each side of her. They slowly began walking around in a circle, as if they were playing a game of merry-go-round. McGovern, looking at me, didn't know what to do. I motioned for him to chill and to let things play out.

Reese, with a straw hat of her own, lowered her head and pulled the hat down tighter against her skull. The brothers thought she did this because she was enjoying the attention they were giving her.

I knew she had done it to hide her growing anger and facial expressions.

"Ooohwee!" John exclaimed. "Dis niggar's one of da finnist I eva seent!"

As if to test the merchandise, Cleophus grabbed her butt. Reese fought against her instincts to knock him to the other side of the universe.

"Yep! And she gat an arse lack a $20 onion!" he screamed in agreement.

"Naw. It's lack she gat two round canttaloops in hur pants! And I lack it."

John looked over at the general. "I dan't knew bat you, McGovran, but eva wance in a whal, I like me a good ole' pass of niggar gal. And dis wun lack mighty good! Ya mind if'n I tak hur inta da woods fur a spell?"

Reese's arms were now twitching out of control. She was about to explode.

Please look at it as a compliment, Reese. When you go back to the present, you can always tell your friends that your booty looks sooo good, it drove White men in 1862 wild!

Luckily, Jeb stepped in to rectify things.

"John, gat yur butt back on dis wagon and leave otha folks niggars alone! Ifn' ya still feel froggy wun we gat home, ya have yur own niggars to jump on!"

The two brothers scattered back on the wagon.

"Ah, Pa," John said in disgust, "ya neva lat me have any fun!"

"I apalgize, McGovran, fur my boys bein' honorary," Jeb told him.

Don't you mean, ornery, you backward, inbred, racist bastard?

McGovern couldn't help but lob another personal attack. He looked back at Reese.

"No offense, taken, Jeb. She DOES have a nice-looking rump. I understand why your son got worked up."

WTF? I didn't have to look at Reese to know she was thinking the same thing as I was.

What a passive-aggressive asshole.

"No," Jeb told him. "My son ned to have his mund on wuk, not on ass! And specially nat no niggars! We bought dese slavs in town and now ned to git dem home, brack in, and put to wuk."

"Well, thanks for letting us know we were headed the right way. We won't take up any more of your time."

With that, Jeb pulled on the reins of the horses and the wagon started inching away. As it passed, both Cleophus and John broke their necks to stare at Reese's butt. When the bound slaves walked by, they looked over at us with a certain sadness in their eyes. It was hard not to look at them and be disgusted by everything. I was a historian who, once upon a time, had the luxury of being able to emotionally detach myself from the most brutal aspects of the past.

Yet seeing the racism and horror of slavery up front personally put me in my feelings and into a malaise of rage. After the wagon and the caravan of slaves had gotten out of earshot, McGovern's nervousness dissipated and he began to gloat.

"Thanks for the advice, Dr. Mazique. We pulled that off without a hitch!"

What kind of doophuny was the general smoking? WE didn't pull off a DAMN thing!

Cluelessly, he continued, "It was almost like every one of you instinctively knew what to do."

Motioning to Porras to begin marching toward Greenville, Nguyen shot McGovern a dirty look.

"Of course, I did. I've been dealing with racist rednecks all of my life."

The general was too slow to understand Nguyen had included him in that statement. Reese, keeping her head down and still saying nothing, started walking behind Porras and him. It wasn't until then that McGovern's attention returned to the stick I had given him.

"By the way," he asked, "what was THIS for?"

Turning to keep up with the others, I said, "Once I saw they had slaves, I understood their mentality. I gave you the stick in case you had to display to them who was boss, so you could beat me with it."

"I still don't understand."

"Slaveholders had to establish and maintain a certain dominance over their slaves. I thought you might enjoy showing off."

"And why would you say that?"

I spoke softly as I scampered to catch up with the others.

"Just a feeling, General McGovern. Just a feeling."

Chapter Seven
the plot thickens

It took the rest of the morning and most of the afternoon for us to reach Greenville. We didn't encounter another group until we came into town. I used the time during our walk to try to get more out of McGovern and to attempt to familiarize myself with Nguyen and Porras.

Knowing she was still simmering from what had occurred earlier, I steered clear of Reese to give her time to deal with her anger issues: Not that I didn't suffer from some of the same problems. I was not used to someone using the N-word, hurling it around with impunity, as if it were their birthright. In the past, whenever anyone White had the temerity to utter it in my presence, I simply socked them in the jaw.

Fortunately, it had been a long time since I had done such a thing. Call it maturity, though even my African American colleagues knew I abhorred the word "nigger" and would look at them sideways every time any of them used it. Although I had encountered some White peers in academia who definitely WANTED to call me the N-word, luckily for their safety, none had. Now, however, I was in an era where being called a nigger was commonplace.

Many Whites during this time looked at Blacks as

less than human and could give zero fucks about their feelings. There was no such thing as bullying or harassment, at least as it pertained to slavocracy. I knew I would have to develop a thicker skin. Reese would SURELY have to develop a thicker skin!

"So, tell me, Dr. Mazique," McGovern asked about 30 minutes after the wagon and the slaves had passed, "what is this thing about equity?"

"Huh?" I responded, not knowing to what he was referring.

He attempted to clarify himself. "In your paper, *Return to Nubia*, part of the question to which you responded was, *If Black people in America could go back in time to make things more equitable in the present...* What did you mean, make things more equitable? Couldn't you have simply said to make things more equal?"

That's a good question! Maybe the general isn't such a dumbass after all.

"Many people think equality and equity are the same things. They aren't, but what's worse is Black people have never had equality, and they damn sure have never had equity. Equality is like me giving everyone the same shoes to wear. Equity is me giving everyone shoes that fit."

"What's the difference?"

Maybe he's not as smart as I thought.

"The difference is not everyone starts off at the

same place. Someone affluent might not need as much as someone poor."

"So, you're implying White America should just give Blacks a blank check every month because they are not as affluent as Whites?"

"Don't be juvenile, General. No one said anything about reparations. Although there IS something to be said about a race of people who worked sun up to sun down for centuries and never received a dime. But that's another conversation for another time.

"You asked me about equity and equality, regarding the thesis statement I responded to in *Return to Nubia*. The simple answer is that I wanted to make sure Black people got their just due. In practically every walk of life, African Americans did not start at the same place as Whites in this nation. If I were going to write a paper about time travel and clandestine assassinations, I was going to make sure Blacks damn well had equity."

"Still sounds like a blank check to me," McGovern mumbled under his breath loud enough for me to hear.

I returned the favor. "I agree...just like the blank check the United States gives out in subsidies every month to all of those White farmers."

He turned and glared. "Are you going to argue with me over every little thing?"

"That depends. Are you going to continue to spew odorous rhetoric of a bovine nature?"

McGovern shook his head in disgust. Seeing he was consumed with irritation, I moved to ask some questions of my own while he was off balance.

"Enough of race and politics," I said. "Let's lighten the mood up. Tell me, assuming we catch up to Major Lewis…"

"Oh, we WILL catch up to Major Lewis, Dr. Mazique. We WILL catch up to Major Lewis."

"Okay, then. WHEN we catch up to Major Lewis, what are you going to do with him?"

McGovern paused. Then he replied, "I can't tell you, Dr. Mazique. That's classified."

"Classified? What do you mean, it's classified? There're only so many things you CAN do with him, and eventually I will know. I AM a part of this group, and when you catch him, you at LEAST have to take him back to the…"

I didn't finish my sentence. There was no need. Instantly, the realization McGovern was going to kill Major Lewis came to me. Part of this was understandable. By now, Lewis was probably considered an enemy of the state, with orders to be eliminated on sight. Or could there be another reason for wanting him dead?

If Lewis had something on McGovern, something extremely detrimental to his career, McGovern might be looking to take Lewis out before he could reveal anything. Disposing of Lewis in the timestream would be a brilliant way to cover up evidence. But if McGovern took out Major Lewis, who else in the group would he also have to take out? We were ALL witnesses. Perhaps this is why he had made sure he was the only White person in the group. How easy would it be for him to leave everyone in the past behind as slaves?

I would have to warn Reese about the potential danger, that is, if she hadn't already figured it out. She came off as pretty smart. Plus, I figured Major Lewis and she were together for a reason. As Reese had stated, they thought alike. She might not be the trained walking force of destruction Lewis was, but she was just as savvy and, in my eyes, just as deadly.

I had to find out where Nguyen and Porras stood. Were they in on things with McGovern, or were they soldiers who would blindly follow orders? I continued with small talk for a few more minutes before I increased my stride toward the two male lieutenants. In doing so, I walked past Reese, who gave me a dirty look, but I took no offense. She was still caught up in her feelings.

Due to the impending danger, I would have taken a few moments to chat, but I didn't want McGovern to know I was onto him. We would strategize later. In my mind, the mission had changed. Major Lewis was still the target, but the reason for reaching him was now more compelling.

Before anything else could happen, Reese and I had to find out what Lewis had on McGovern. What was it about the General that had made him so paranoid? Why had he snapped and gone into the timestream to change the past? What imminent threat had compelled him to do so?

Nguyen was more cordial than Porras. He smiled at me while Porras continued to snarl. By now, I had caught up to them and we were far enough ahead of McGovern that he couldn't hear our conversation.

"Sorry about that back there," I said to Nguyen, trying to open up the conversation. "I shouldn't have put you two in that situation, but I didn't know what else to say to use as a cover that would have made any sense."

Nguyen waved his hand, dismissing the incident. "Don't be sorry," he enthusiastically replied. "What you did was brilliant! The story you gave was the only one that would have worked. It's not YOUR fault we're stuck in a period where we can't be our true selves. Besides, I saw ALL of the *Rush Hours* movies when I was a kid. I KNOW how to act like an ignorant Chinaman."

He paused before doing his best Jackie Chan impression with a heavy Asian accent.

"Can you undastand the words that are coming outta my mouth?"

We all started laughing.

"No, Dr. Mazique," Nguyen continued, "don't apologize for what happened. I've been dealing with racist White people all of my life. So have my mother and father. They were first-generation Chinese who came here to America and carved out a life of their own. While THEY speak with a heavy Asian accent, I don't. They beat the King's English into me perfectly so I would better fit in.

"Funny thing is, it never quite worked out that way. I was teased about my race all through public school. I've been called everything from the Karate Kid to Chopsticks and Hong Kong Phooey. I joined the military to pay for school and to become a part of, and give to, this country."

Nguyen's story about his family, while touching, escaped me. I was focused on what he had said about his accent. When I had first met him, I had never thought about it: There was no hint of ANY type of foreign accent in his speech, Asian or otherwise. He enunciated all of his words perfectly as if he were a wine-drinking, bourgeoisie Stanford graduate who had a stick up his ass.

I motioned to Porras, knowing he could hear me.

"What's HIS story?"

Porras gave me a dirty look.

Nguyen responded, "Who? Him?" He glanced back at his teammate and smiled.

"I don't think he likes me that much," I stated, wanting Porras to react. He did, just not in the way

I expected. A wry grin began to appear across his face.

"Why do you say that?" Nguyen asked. "Because he doesn't speak much?"

Porras and I stared at each other at the same time.

"Yeah, something like that," I mused.

"Don't worry. If he didn't like you, he would talk your ear off."

That doesn't make much sense.

"Maybe I didn't hear you right."

"No, you heard me right. If Porras didn't like or trust you, he would be fake and talk your ear off about nothing in particular just to irritate and drive you the hell away from him."

Interesting. Maybe I'll use that strategy with McGovern.

Porras and I continued to have a staring contest.

"Okay, I get the silent treatment," I told Nguyen, "but why does he persist in scowling at me?"

For the first time since meeting him, Porras broke character, stopped glaring, and spoke.

With a slight Mexican accent, he said, "It's an old battle technique to see how your adversary reacts."

"Really?" I retorted. "How did I do?"

"Better than I thought you would, for a gringo, anyway; or, in your case, a civilian. You MIGHT make it through this mission."

Nguyen and he began chuckling.

I began laughing with them, happy I had finally broken through Porras' cold demeanor, even if I was the butt of his joke. At least he was talking now.

"Thank you for the vote of confidence."

I paused strategically before asking, "Tell me, gentlemen, what is YOUR assessment of this mission?"

I thought Nguyen would be the first to speak. I was wrong.

"This whole thing stinks like a big mound of doo-doo," Porras fumed. "We were told Major Lewis entered the timestream with several other soldiers but were only briefed about him, and so far, we've only been focused on him. What about the others? What about their background information?"

I knew that was a lie almost as soon as I had figured out Lewis' long game. The discussion at Starbucks that day didn't focus on sending back many people to the past. This was the beauty of my plan. Since there were not a myriad of targets to eliminate, it only called for one person to complete the mission. If Lewis had stuck with the rest of the plan, he would have entered the timestream by himself. He was more than capable of eliminating Booth and Johnson with ease.

Nguyen interrupted Porras. "You also forgot to add the fact there is something utterly bogus about McGovern. Despite the fact he is an arsehole, why is a general—brigadier or not—even on a mission like this? He was quite insistent that he lead this command. Funny thing is, I don't know if he actually received clearance to do so before we left. There were a couple of lower-ranked officers who were supposed to head this excursion—some infinitely more battle-hardened who get off on this sort of thing—but were left behind."

I looked over at them. "So, what are you two saying?"

Porras briefly eyeballed Nguyen before slickly chiming in, "I think I can speak for my brotha from another motha. This whole situation is gonna end up FUBAR!"

A little later during our stroll toward Greenville, I had worked my way back towards Reese. She was heading up the rear of our little excursion and it wasn't because she couldn't keep up the pace. Rather, she had purposely positioned herself there to keep from having to talk to anyone. I knew she was still pissed, but it was time for us to talk.

With a hint of an attitude still in her voice, before I was able to utter a word, she asked, "Did you have fun talking to my two comrades?"

"Yes, we bonded quite beautifully. It was a wonderful sight to see. You should have been there."

"Sorry, I was too busy getting over the trauma of having my ass fondled by the two hillbillies from *Green Acres*!"

"God, do I miss that show!"

"What did you say?"

I guess now was not the time to reminiscence?

All jokes aside, I saw I was going to have to hit Reese with some hard truths.

"First, let me say how truly sorry I am you had to endure that, but you're going to HAVE to lose the attitude and get over it."

Venom came from her lips. "Who do you think you're talking to?"

"I'm talking to you, First Lieutenant Reese! Black women have put up with MORE than a simple ass grab for you to be where you are today. We have a mission to complete and questions to be answered. Act emotionally and you blow all of that. Trust me, I overstand you being mad because of what happened, but thank God that's ALL that happened. Get over it and let's move on."

Reese shot daggers out of her eyes a few seconds more before her facial expression softened. She nodded her head.

"You're right," she finally said. "Besides...there's something I need to tell you."

She glanced ahead at McGovern to make sure he wasn't eavesdropping. Then she whispered, "We're being followed."

I couldn't help but look around behind us.

"I don't see anyone."

"Trust me, you wouldn't. That's how good he is."

"How good WHO is?"

"Major Lewis."

This time, I stopped walking and slowly did a full 360-degree turn. When I still didn't see anything out of the ordinary, I resumed my walk.

"You sure you're not just being hopeful?" I questioned.

"Maybe," Reese conceded, "but for some reason, I've always been able to sense him before he was there."

"Perhaps you two are soulmates after all. Or perhaps you're just imagining things. At any rate, your comrades don't seem to like or trust your boss any more than either of us."

"Does that surprise you?"

"No, but what DID surprise me was what McGovern told me he was going to do with Major Lewis when we caught up to him."

A look of concern overcame Reese's face. "What did he say?"

"He didn't. He told me it was classified."

She thought about it for a moment.

"That means he plans to kill him to prevent having to take him back."

"Yes. I came to the same conclusion. I also came to the conclusion that his doing so doesn't set a proper example for a United States general. He will also have to do something with us, the witnesses."

I paused

"Tell me, just what does Lewis have over McGovern to push him to such lengths?"

Reese glanced at me, before stating, "Now you have me asking that same question."

Chapter Eight
introspection

The trail the group was on eventually turned into a well-worn dirt path leading into town. Along the way, there came to be a growing scattering of houses and assorted businesses. While some curious Whites took the time to gaze at us, most were too busy or too far away to pay any attention. Porras and Nguyen might have been strange-looking to them, but being close to a major thoroughfare, the inhabitants were probably used to a wide assortment of passersby, especially since Tennessee was still a slave state.

Though I would like to say I was calm and composed, in truth on the inside I was as nervous as a whore at a Southern Baptist Convention. The full reality of my present situation came to me in another sudden epiphany. I was a Black man from the present now in the past. Not just at ANY time in American history, but in 1862, a time when many felt justified keeping my people subservient.

When our group had first exited the portal, if we had encountered any adversity under the cover of darkness, I was more than confident we would have come out on top. Though not heavily armed, we had enough light modern weaponry and ammunition to mount a proper defense to escape into the woods at night. But now?   It was daylight and we were headed into a highly populated area. If something bad occurred, there was no cover of darkness under which to hide. There would also be more people to fight. Modern weaponry aside, there was no way we could indefinitely hold out against superior numbers.

I shuddered to think of what would happen to me, a Black man in the South, if captured. It's not like the U.S. military in the present had given me papers showing I was a freedman. I turned back and looked at Reese. Her fate would be worse than mine and that knowledge gave me no remorse. If anything, it only highlighted my concerns, making me more antsy. I thought back to the beginning of the introduction I always gave at the initial meeting of my classes and found myself being a hypocrite.

***

"Hello, everyone. I see we have a packed house this morning! I feel honored. My name is Dr. Mazique. Welcome to the first session. If you haven't stabbed anyone or gotten into a fight after the conclusion of this class, I hope you will find what you're about to hear interesting enough to return and learn more of."

A young, tall, nicely coiffed Black kid in the lecture hall quickly raised his hand.

"Yes, sir?"

"Um," the student hesitated, "why would anyone stab someone or get into a fight after this?"

They ALWAYS take the bait.

"Because…. I'm sorry. What's your name?"

"Jeremy."

"Well, Jeremy, I made that statement because knowledge is a dangerous thing. While it does make one more aware, sometimes it can also make one angry. Resentful. Even vengeful. During our first meeting, I want to address and confront the elephants in the room. I also want to establish class norms and how we will handle situations when discussions get tense."

"And you think what we will learn in this class will make us tense?"

A wicked grin overcame my face.

"Most of you?" I strategically paused to look out at their young faces if only to build a silent crescendo. "No. But for some…. There are those who live in glass houses, on tracts of land with white picket fences, birds chirping in the background, and apple pies in their hands. THEY are the ones who will be shocked at what has supposedly been kept from them."

Jeremy's face contorted and I sensed a bit of rebel in his soul. I already liked him. I could tell he would be among the seeming few in class who would challenge me. For now, however, I had to establish dominance.

90

I was already countering what I knew he would say. He was assertive in his attack.

"First and foremost, why shouldn't someone be shocked to learn they have been lied to all of their life?" Jeremy asked. "And what do you mean by 'has supposedly been kept from us'? You teach Black history. You KNOW what's been kept from us!"

You are like the young bull who runs down and scares the herd.

I smiled and was calm with my rebuke. "Well, Jeremy, I hate to answer a question WITH a question, but has anyone REALLY been lied to, or have they simply been presented with one perspective? If so, whose fault is it that they didn't seek to learn a DIFFERENT perspective? During slavery, many Blacks died making an effort to read and write because it was against the law.

"What is the excuse now? As you stated, first and foremost, we BOTH know what Black people are up against. It's ludicrous to think the oppressor is going to provide us with an uplifting narrative. We need to stop being lazy and seek knowledge for ourselves."

I hit a nerve. Jeremy became agitated. "You think Black people are lazy?"

"Not Black people specifically, just anyone with that sort of mentality. Stop giving the system more credit than it deserves.

"Frederick Douglass basically taught himself how to read and write. Now, we have Black recalcitrants, like R. Kelly, who are functionally illiterate pedophiles, and you want to blame everything on someone else? Go figure. Schools are littered with kids who can recite every word to *Bump and Grind* but can't spell it."

Jeremy's eyes began to bulge from their sockets. I could tell he wanted to leap from his seat. Still, I couldn't resist the urge to goad him a little more. While I had never pissed off a student enough to take a swing at me—most weren't that crazy—I was more than prepared to beat the brakes off anyone who became froggy enough to try.

Yet I also felt I had a responsibility to teach my students how to reel in their emotions, to overcome the pain of the past, so they could better understand it. This scenario was the beginning of that process.

"Who are YOU to talk about Black people like that?" Jeremy roared.

The rest of the class began looking at each other, becoming disturbed by the clash of fiery rhetoric. "Aren't you supposed to be a history professor? What are you REALLY a professor of? *Blaming the Victim for the Crime 101*?"

I smiled again, but this time it was an *I-told-you-so* grin. I hesitated a little longer before finally offering a calming critique.

"Jeremy, if that's how you handle a simple tête-à-tête, how are you going to react when we talk about the horrors of the slave trade? When you learn how Africans were packed like sardines and shackled down below in the belly of slave ships? They had to lay in their own excrement, while lice crawled over them and rats gnawed on their dead comrades. Are you going to become enraged then too?"

I hesitated.

"What are you going to do when we review **State of Missouri v. Celia, a Slave**? In 1849, Celia was a slave in Missouri who had been bought by Robert Newsome, whose wife had recently died. Celia was 14 years old at the time she was purchased. Newsome couldn't even wait until he got her back home to Calloway County before he raped her. As a matter of fact, during a five-year period, he habitually assaulted her. In fact, he raped her SO much that the man she came to love, another slave named George, stopped having anything to do with her. One day in 1850, Newsome told Celia he was going to come to her cabin that night.

"She knew what he wanted and warned him against it. She was pregnant again. Newsome didn't care and didn't pay her any mind. She ended up killing him and tried to burn the body in the fireplace. When she was put on trial, her lawyer attempted to claim self-defense.

"After all, women had a right to protect themselves against rape, right? It was ruled Celia couldn't claim rape because she was a slave and slaves were property. Like animals. And sometimes, unfortunately, animals attack their masters and have to be put down. Of course, that last part is an oversimplification. Celia was allowed to live long enough to produce a stillborn child. She was quickly hung thereafter."

There was another hesitation on my part, this time more than a few seconds in duration. I looked at Jeremy. His face began to soften. It was only then he realized he had proven my point.

"I'm sorry, Dr. Mazique. I guess I just got caught up in my feelings," he finally uttered.

"No offense taken, but now you see why I said what I said at the beginning of class. I can tell you know some African American history and you probably think you're pretty well-grounded. But I've got to know all of you aren't going to start yelling at each other once we start discussing something really deep."

"You mean **State of Missouri v. Celia, a Slave** isn't considered something really deep?" someone asked out loud.

That devilish grin once more overcame my face. "No. That's just surface-level stuff. We're going to be like Jacques Cousteau and dive REALLY deep!"

"So," a Latino female student in front of the class

started to wonder, "are you saying we SHOULDN'T get mad at the things we're going to learn in this class? I'm seeing now that might be kind of hard."

I shook my head. "No, I'm not saying that. I'm simply stating not to become so consumed by your anger—by something you can't change—that you become blinded to the forest for the trees. Let me switch gears for a minute and come from a different angle. How many of you like omelets?"

"What kind are we talking about?" Jeremy questioned light heartedly. "Ham and cheese?"

"Let's just say, how many of you like any omelet of your choice?"

Practically everyone raised their hands.

"Good. I feel the same way. But unfortunately, the PROCESS of making one...well, it's really brutal. You have to break some eggs, pour in some ingredients, and whisk them around. If you think about it, America is like that omelet. It had to break some things. It stole people, committed genocide, and robbed others of land. Along the way, it was both hypocritical and contradictory.

"However, despite the brutality, when an omelet is finally finished, it's a work of art, a tantalizing delight to the tastebuds. This country is the same. It has transcended its beginning, just like those broken eggs that were turned into an omelet.

"This class isn't about making anyone feel bad

about themself. It's about fully embracing our past so we can properly inform our future. We can't go back and change things, but we can improve on them. If you don't like the taste of the ingredients of the omelet now sitting on your plate in America, don't simply bitch about it. Work to improve your knowledge of self and the recipe to give birth to a better omelet!"

***

Now that shit was real—me being in the past, facing the potential death and adversities my ancestors faced—I was embarrassed I had ever told my students to rein in their emotions. How could I ask them to do what I presently couldn't? Despite me thinking I was doing an adequate job not outwardly showing the terror coursing through my veins, the facade was not good enough to deter Reese. She noticed something amiss.

Attempting to speak only loud enough for the two of us to communicate, she asked, "You alright?"

"Did my facial expressions give it away? I would lie to you and say yes, but you appear to have your fiancé's knack for surveillance. I think my area of expertise makes me both a liability AND an asset emotionally."

"What do you mean?"

"I know about American history better than any of you: Every crack and crevice. Because of this, I'm more aware of everything that happened—everything that CAN happen—and I guess that knowledge has my paranoia working overtime."

Reese tried to assuage my fears. "Well, I've been thinking things over. McGovern would have a hard time betraying us. We are ALL from anyone here's future. He can't reveal us as interlopers without revealing himself. Any person from this time period—White OR Black—would look at us as if we were three-headed stepchildren who only had 10 chromosomes."

"Maybe, but McGovern is White. In this time period, being a White man from the future is different than being a person of color from the future. How they react to him will be completely different from how they react to us, particularly if McGovern controls the narrative."

"Would anyone in this state even consider the narrative from a person of color?" Reese asked.

We looked at each other and silently came to the same chilling conclusion. We would have to be vigilant to monitor what McGovern said to any White person with whom we came into contact. There might come a time when Reese or I might have to kill him if he attempted to double-cross us. And for some reason, I was more comfortable with that thought than I should have been.

Chapter Nine
closer to the truth

The group made it to Greenville, Tennessee, sometime after 1600 hours. Since I was growing tired of not referring to time using AM and PM as civilians normally do, I began questioning the significance of using military time. Nguyen explained it was something put into practice in the United Kingdom during World War I.

Because the military operated 24 hours a day, seven days a week, it began using the 24-hour timetable to avoid confusion between AM and PM hours. While I felt foolish for not knowing this tidbit of information, I tried not to be too hard on myself. Despite being a historian, I couldn't know EVERY damn thing! For instance, I still don't know which came first, the chicken or the egg. So, what kind of historian does that really make me?

However, what I DO know is that despite my paranoia, I was totally, absolutely in my element when the group made it into town. My eyes widened as I tried to take in everything: The ambiance, the movement of the people, the vibe, and the temperament of the times. What I had only seen in pictures was now in living color right before me. Even the replicas of historic buildings back in the present surely could not be as authentic as the ones I was now seeing in the past.

Yes, I know, the present-past thing sometimes STILL gets confusing. *Get over yourself and roll with it.* My point is, experiencing everything—not having to rely on old newspapers or narratives from the past—was no substitute for being in the actual period. The whole experience was like an orgasm of information and I had yet to reach a climax.

Since the streets were more crowded and we were closer in proximity to the populace, we attracted more attention than before. More specifically, the White people we walked by began staring at Nguyen and Porras incessantly.

"We need to get off the street," I advised McGovern in a low voice, "but we also need to find someplace we can gather information."

"Agreed," he replied. A couple of moments later, I saw our salvation.

I pointed ahead in the direction we were already headed. "There's a courthouse," I said. The rest of the group focused their attention on a building in the distance which was larger and fancier than the others. The words, *"Greenville County Courthouse"*, were painted on a sign at the top.

McGovern issued a backhanded compliment if it could even be called that. "Nice find, Dr. Mazique, but it kind of goes against your nature."

I smell some bovine defecation coming, but I'll bite.

"Oh? And what nature is that?"

"The natural revulsion for anything toward having to do with authority.

Did this two-bit Gomer Pyle just say what I THINK he said?

"No, I just have a natural revulsion to any policeman that would put a bullet in my ass simply because I'm Black. But to your point, you ARE right: I seem to have the same aversion to authority the people who stormed the capital on January sixth had."

Uppercut! I could tell he was flummoxed by that statement.

He huffed, "Some would say those were patriots."

I shook my head. "You really want to do this right now while we're walking toward the courthouse? Fine. One man's patriot is another man's terrorist...but I guess that depends on one's perspective...or one's skin color."

"Don't get defensive with me, Doctor! My people aren't the ones always begging money for social programs or to defund the police."

"Only probably because YOUR people are too busy orchestrating Enron and the **Savings and Loan Crisis**."

That must have hit a nerve. McGovern stopped in his tracks and turned to face me.

"You're pushing it, Dr. Mazique," he said, pointing a finger in my face. "Remember what period we're in."

He glared for another second before resuming his walk. *I think McGovern just told me who in this group is the real HNIC!*

I could feel Reese and the others staring at the back of my head, trying to figure out what was going on between us. They couldn't hear the exact conversation, but could see my body language, which I had to immediately relax. It wouldn't end well for the rest of the group if the crowd perceived me as challenging a White man.

This is, in part, why I hadn't responded to McGovern's last statement. His sarcasm wasn't difficult to supersede; he wasn't that smart. Yet my interest was in winning the time war rather than the petty battle of rhetoric between him and me. That would come later. I was sure of it. Besides, I fully intended on letting Reese have a bite of McGovern's ass before taking any recompense.

There were a lot of people—all White—milling in and out of the courthouse. No one in our group really paid this any mind, and why should we? Although we knew we were in the past, we still had present-day sensibilities. When it was evident all five of us were seeking entry into the courthouse, we were abruptly brought crashing back to reality. There were a couple of hillbilly-looking types standing outside who began leering at us as if we had just robbed a church.

Walking behind McGovern, carrying his knapsack, I was second in line. When the general began his assent up a set of stairs to enter the building, a big, burly White man stepped behind him to block my path.

"Niggas ain't 'llowed in da courthouse," he said with a deep, country twang, looking me up and down. "You gonna have ta leave ya niggas outside, mista, whale ya tac care of business."

I was fuming inside because I couldn't retaliate and had to take the verbal abuse.

I got your nigga hanging in between my legs, asshole! You probably couldn't SPELL nigga even if I gave you the letters.

Another man who had been standing outside asked McGovern, "You from 'round here, mista?"

McGovern looked at me for a second. My facial expression told him he was on his own. These guys didn't seem to tolerate a slave speaking for his master. I had thought all hope was lost. McGovern was taking too long to respond.

Finally, he said, "My name is McGovern and I'm a judge from Little Rock, Arkansas, here on business before I head to Chapel Hill and Pulaski County, Tennessee."

Despite being on high alert, I became even more so when I heard the words Chapel Hill and Pulaski County, Tennessee, come from out of the general's mouth. The expression on my face must also have been one of astonishment because Reese suddenly stared at me, trying to figure out why McGovern's words had visibly vexed me. Again, I had to rein in my emotions and relax to avoid drawing any attention to myself. Slaves were supposed to be compliant and obedient. Like dogs.

A third hillbilly told McGovern, "You cane leave ya' niggas here, mista. We ain't gonna steal 'em frome ya!"

"No," the first one interjected, beginning to laugh, "but dis dang war sho might!" They all three burst out into a loud guffaw. I could see Reese's arm beginning to twitch.

"I'm sho whateva ya lookin' fo, ya can find inside," big and burly continued to say before pointing at McGovern's pistol on his hip. "But ya' gonna have ta check ya sidepace, mista, when ya go inside."

"No problem, McGovern told them before turning toward me.

"Make sure you're somewhere I don't have to come looking for all of you," he commanded in a very assertive tone of voice before continuing his ascent up the stairs and going inside.

Was that last part for show? McGovern was acting a little TOO real, if you ask me.

There was an eerie moment of silence as the three men glared at us. Since McGovern's verbal actions had marked me as the designated leader of the group—the current HNIC—I slowly motioned for the group to move away from the three men and to the side of the building. They began following my lead, but then one of them pointed at Nguyen.

"You lack kinda funny. Whet kinda nigga is ya?" he questioned. This led to closer scrutiny from the other two men. All three boldly walked up to us. I could see Reese reaching for her pistol in her rucksack, but I shook my head, making a hand gesture for her to remain calm.

I know you want to pop a plug in their asses, Reese, I thought, *but...PLEASE...just CHILL!*

"Wherein ya frome, boy?" the man questioned Nguyen again. Even though I could see in the second lieutenant's eyes he didn't know what to say, to his credit, he didn't panic, even as the other men surrounded him.

Big and burly yelled, "Cat gat ya tong, boy? Spake when a White mane spakes to ya!"

Suddenly, I was inclined to tell Reese to let a couple of bullets fly. The air instantly became tense. However, Nguyen being Nguyen, having dealt with a lifetime of racial and social abuse, was unfortunately well-experienced with such situations. Keeping his composure, he simply relied on his tried-and-true anti-racist routine: He feigned ignorance.

Bucking out his eyes, he said in a heavy Asian

accent, "Me speaka no English." Then, as if no one had heard him, he uttered the catchphrase once more: "Me speaka no English!"

The White men, perhaps expecting a different reaction, were paralyzed due to their inability to respond. Cocking their heads sideways, seemingly in unison, their angry demeanor lessened into more of a cursory nature. Now they began viewing Nguyen with amazement.

"I know whatcha is," one of the men retorted as if the second lieutenant were some sort of prize cow. "He's whatca call a Chinaman!"

Another one of the men's eyes widened. "Yas, I hurd of 'em. Got 'em workin' on da railrad. Betta dem dan me. I hurd dat wos some hurd wurk! And dangerose, too!"

"Ya, rat. Betta a Chinaman dan me. White mane shadn't do wurk like dat. Wurk like dat is for niggas."

"Or Chinamain!" one of the men exclaimed before all began chuckling together again.

"Whale, whatevea ya'll is, niggas or Chinamain, ya'll jus wait fo ya masta, like he sade. And dan't do no phony business. We lack our niggas doin' as de told 'round hur. Jus 'cause dis war goin' on, dan't mean nothin'. We hang uppity niggas...and Chinamain 'round hur."

I was furious I had to be quiet and compliant, but

I also found old habits hard to break. I had already sized the men up. In my mind, I knew who I was going to hit first and how I was going to knock the other two out. I didn't need any of the group's help in doing so, either.

Yet I couldn't resort to my fists. They would place us all in danger and jeopardize the mission. My ancestors often had to be patient and compliant as they stealthily planned to overcome adversities placed before them. I would have to do the same.

Bending slightly over to show humility, I replied in my best Kunta Kinte voice, "Yessa, we undastand, sur. Yessa, we undastand."

Motioning to the others, I quickly ushered them away and to the side of the building. Once out of earshot, we began to talk amongst ourselves.

"I know ONE thing," Reese let out, "I'm tired of this bullshit! Let someone else say the word 'nigga'. One. More. Time!"

"Control yourself, Reese," I pleaded, looking around to see if anyone had heard her outburst.

"Control myself? Out of the four of us, I think I'm the only one who will get called a nigga AND have her ass grabbed at the same time, so please, don't tell me to control myself!"

I gently snatched her up and looked into her eyes.

"Reese, if you don't get ahold of yourself, you're

going to blow our cover. Then you'll have a lot MORE to worry about than getting called a nigga and having your ass grabbed."

"Personally," Nguyen chimed in, his fake Asian accent gone, "I'm having the time of my life! Who knew White people could be so gullible?"

Porras gave him an odd look. "Only you could find humor in racism."

Nguyen shrugged his shoulders. "That's what's wrong with America. Too sensitive nowadays."

"You DO realize that when you say nowadays," Porras told him, "you are actually referring to our present and their future? Technically, we're sort of in limbo. We are not in OUR present, but we are not of their PAST either."

Nguyen paused and glanced at him before responding, "I think I like it better when you go around acting all glum and gloomy. An Aztec warrior!"

"Is that your way of telling me to shut up?"
"Yes."

I could see the frustration on Reese's face. Nguyen's and Porras' banter wasn't making things any better either. I moved to offer counsel.

"It's not like I'm NOT pissed off at everything that's happening, Reese. Believe me, I wanted to put paws on those guys, too, but this mission isn't about me or us. It's about humanity. I have to admit, though, I haven't heard the N-word hurled with such impunity since Rudy Ray Moore's *The Human Tornado*."

I knew those words didn't offer much comfort, but I could tell she appreciated the effort. Her mind and demeanor switched gears.

"What did McGovern say to you that had you puzzled?" she asked.

Her changing vibe took me by surprise. "Huh?"

"Before McGovern had gone into the courthouse, he was giving those assholes his itinerary. What did he say that alarmed you?"

I coyly asked, "What makes you think I was alarmed?"

"Because you looked like it."

Damn, this woman is good. Why don't we just let HER do surveillance?

I hesitated if only to give myself time to put words in context for a proper explanation.

"This mission just keeps getting weirder and weirder. And maybe this just happens to be a coincidence, but..."

Now, Nguyen and Porras were listening intently.

"Go on," Porras urged.

"Do any of you know who Nathan Bedford Forest was/is? This damn time travel is confusing."

They all looked at one another and shook their heads.

"No? You mean, NONE of you have EVER heard of this guy? What kind of history classes did you have in high school?"

Reese answered defensively, "Obviously not the kind that taught African American history."

"Well, this isn't BLACK history, Cantaloupe booty, it's WHITE history of the most sordid kind."

She shot me a dirty look. I guess she didn't like my sarcastic dig at her gluteus maximus. Well, if she didn't like it now, she surely wasn't to like things later. If the group made it back, I was going to make sure it became her new nickname.

"Okay. Let me ask all of you another question. Maybe it will tie in all of this. Have any of you ever heard of the Ku Klux Klan?"

Porras said some cuss words in Spanish. Nguyen replied, "I'm Asian and even I have heard of the KKK!"

Reese inquired, "What does that have to do with this Bedford guy?"

"He's the one who help found the organization," I retorted matter-of-factly, "December 24, 1865, to be exact."

If I didn't have it before, I now had their full, undivided attention.

"Okay, it's time for the next question. Guess where the Klan was formed?"

Nguyen struggled to remember McGovern's conversation. "Pulaski County?"

"Bingo! Okay. Now, where do you think Bedford was born?"

Reese uttered, "Chapel Hill?"

"You're cooking with fire, Reese. Now, you're cooking with fire."

Porras voiced another loud Spanish obscenity.

"One last thing. I think I may be coming to understand why your fiancé was investigating General McGovern."

Nguyen and Porras started looking at me oddly and Reese instantly became incensed I had betrayed her trust.

"What do you mean, McGovern was being investigated?" Porras asked.

I ignored him and stopped Reese before she could get started.

"Look, I know what you told me was supposed to be kept secret," I rationalized with her, "but I think it's time for the four of us to lay all of our cards on the table. I have a feeling we're going to need each other if we're going to make it through this mission."

I gave Reese a few seconds to think about what I said. Several moments later, she nodded her head in quiet acquiescence.

I turned to Porras and Nguyen. "We will fill you in fully on everything later. For now, just listen to what I'm about to say. When McGovern and I stopped in the street as we were walking over here, we were…debating, for lack of a better word, as we have been doing. He didn't like what I was saying, so he threatened me."

"What do you mean, he threatened you?" Reese asked.

"I mean just that: He threatened me. He told me to remember the period I was in. I noticed his already bad disposition turned worse when I lobbed a jab about January sixth and White people storming the nation's capital. He referred to the participating recalcitrants as patriots. I found that odd for him, as someone who was a military career person, to say."

Now it was Nguyen's time to wonder. "So, what are you saying?"

"I'm just attempting to put the puzzle together. This might be a stretch—and I'm no conspiracy theorist—but…"

"Just say it," Reese egged.

"We have a brigadier general, Nathan Bedford Forest, the Ku Klux Klan, a time machine, AND a renegade major. This same major was secretly investigating McGovern, who has no business being here but somehow attached himself to this mission."

I let that sink in as we all morosely pondered for longer than we should have. Reese finally broke the silence.

"So, what do you think we should do?"

How did I suddenly come to be in charge? You are the ones in the military! I barely have a handle on history and now you want me to be General Benjamin O. Davis, Jr.!

"We play it like you and I talked earlier, Reese. We monitor what McGovern says around White people to make sure he doesn't double-cross us."

"Yeah, but what about times like now?" Porras challenged. "The way this era is about minorities, we might not have much luck watching him all the time."

I thought about that for a second. "True. Then we will just have to also monitor his actions."

I looked at Nguyen and Porras. "Look. I'm not asking or telling you guys to go against your orders or betray your country. I'm just trying to make sure we all stay alert so we can SAVE our country and the world. Something doesn't add up with McGovern. I'm just wondering if we can count on you two if things turn sour."

They glanced at one another before turning back towards me.

"Count me in," Nguyen replied. I've never liked General Custer anyway."

"General Custer?"

Porras clarified, "That's his name for McGovern."

"Oh. And...what about you? Are YOU in?"

"I'm in."

"Good."

People of color. United. It was a hallmark moment that should have made my butt cheeks clench and me all tingly on the inside. Why, then, didn't it? If this had happened, I would have had a stronger resolve, but I didn't. Instead of moving towards collective efficacy, I felt the group was moving backwards with diffidence toward a black hole.

Chapter Ten
the box that forrest made

Nathan Bedford Forrest. The man had always been an enigma to me, not so much because he helped to start the first terrorist hate group in America, but because he had been capable of so much more. Born to a poor family July 13, 1821, he was the eldest of 12 children. Forrest would only receive one year of formal education. During that time, though, he supposedly was more interested in wrestling other students than in instruction.

Years later, in 1845, he would survive his first heated physical fight when he attempted to help his uncle, Johnathan, during a business dispute gone wrong with the Matlock brothers. Forrest's uncle was killed in the melee, but Forrest shot and wounded two men with two separate pistols before wounding two more with a knife.

His reputation was he was a man of dignity and honor; a chivalrous southern gentleman who did not drink, was always dapper, and was quite respectful to the ladies. Soft-spoken most of the time, he could turn into a raging beast if someone pissed him off to the height of pisstivity itself. He eventually became a successful businessman who made most of his money through slavery in one fashion or another, although he also dabbled in farming and speculating.

Yet his primary business is where part of the enigma around him lives. His personal slaves supposedly liked him! But, of course, liking a slave master is not necessarily the same as LIKING a slave master. Some had reputations for beating their slaves more frequently and harsher than others. Put in this context, a person can see why a slave could like or, rather, prefer one slave master over another. The last thing probably giving Forrest street credibility with his personal slaves was he supposedly didn't break up families, which was a common occurrence. By the time the Civil War broke out, Forrest boasted a personal fortune worth $1.5 million.

He returned from Mississippi—where he had been on business ventures—to Tennessee to volunteer for the Confederate army June 14, 1861. Though he enlisted as a private, he was promoted to lieutenant colonel, in part because of his wealth. He eventually became a general and he was quite adept, so much so that Robert E. Lee once called him the greatest soldier of the war. While I have to overlook Lee's obvious bias, I do have to admit he was pretty damn good in battle. Utilizing weapons as leads in cavalry charges, he helped to revolutionize cavalry tactics. He was also one tough bastard.

Twenty-nine horses had been shot out from underneath him during the Civil War. While surviving all of these occurrences was remarkable, he also killed a total of 30 men in hand-to-hand combat. ***The Battle of Fort Pillow*** was perhaps Forrest's most infamous act. In this skirmish alone, he had two horses in quick succession shot out from underneath him. Forrest's men under his command gained the upper hand and overran the fort.

The Union army, armed with approximately 300 White soldiers and 300 Black soldiers, attempted to flee. Many were captured or surrendered. Interestingly, while only a third of White Union soldiers were killed, two-thirds of Black soldiers perished. There were reports abounding of Black soldiers who, on their knees, pleaded with the Confederates soldiers for their lives, only to be bayonetted in the back or stabbed somewhere else on their body. The massacre was so appalling it motivated old Honest Abe to call a special cabinet meeting on how the North should respond.

To his enemies, Forrest became a symbol of evil. Of him, General William Tecumseh Sherman once said, *"Forrest is the devil. . .I will order them [two of his officers] to make up a force and go out to follow Forrest to the death if it costs ten thousand lives and breaks the Treasury. There will never be peace in Tennessee until Forrest is dead!"*

It seems Sherman felt about Forrest the same way I feel about General McGovern. *At least Forrest had stones made of steel. McGovern probably has marbles made of dust.*

Enough squirreling. Let me focus and get back on topic. Where was I? Oh, yes, Forrest...

After the war, Forrest was left destitute. It shattered his business empire. Understandably, he retreated into his anger, mad at Reconstruction and Radical Republicans, believing northern politicians were attempting to penalize the South because it had had the audacity to rebel. Sometime during the spring of 1866, he joined the Klan, which had been started the previous winter by six Confederate veterans of the war. Forrest holds the hideous distinction of being the first Grand Wizard of the Klan.

Unfortunately, he would also become the first to greet Black men in 1868 at the ballot box, leading groups of Klan members in their harassment, of intimidation, and of violence, attempting to prevent them from casting ballots. Years later, however, Forrest would find himself doing something uncharacteristic for a southern White man, particularly one who had been the first Grand Wizard of the KKK: He recanted his evil ways.

Perhaps because he had come to his senses, or perhaps because he saw the destruction the organization was wreaking, in 1869 he abruptly resigned his post and ordered all Klan uniforms to be burned. Forrest would even later claim he had never been an official member of the KKK.

All I know is, if a Black man would have tried to flip the script like that, there would still be an asterisk next to his name in the dictionary with the word DUMBASS underneath in small print.

Forrest also tried to say he had not been anti-Black, only anti-Republican.

Come on, really? This is sort of like shooting a gun randomly in a crowd and, after someone gets hit, claiming the person got in the way of the bullet.

Though it was for political gain, the Radical Republicans had aligned themselves with the Black vote. No organization, group, or person could attack one without invariably attacking the other.

Whatever the case, the group Forrest helped to gaslight during his brief tenure as the Grand Wizard spread like wildfire. Apparently, there were a plethora of southern White men—far less refined and less kind to their slaves—who felt the same way he had. What was worse, they appeared angrier and less repentant. Scores of Blacks were terrorized and brutalized. In the South, it was not uncommon to see Black men hanging from trees, sometimes with their testicles removed!

Talk about a low blow!

In addition to promulgating copycat acts of violence against people of color, the Klan helped to usher in the existence of copycat hate groups like Neo Nazis, Skinheads, and the Proud Boys, the new kids on the block.

Why does a bunch of men who supposedly shed so much testosterone refer to themselves as boys? I keep telling people there's more to that story.

Regarding Forrest and the Klan, I always think about what drives a person to hate; I mean, REALLY hate? Men in the organization called themselves Christians. In fact, one of the requirements in myriad Klan clusters was the belief in God. This begs the question: How could people who called themselves Christians abhor others simply because their skin was different or because they spoke a different way? Does the soul have a color? Does God?

If so, somebody better get McGovern to lie down. God created man in his image and the remains of the first human ever recorded were verified as being in Africa. He might not like where my logic goes...

McGovern's and my differences aside, it would be extremely hard for me to detest someone because of their skin color.

Although I have to be real here: If someone were funky and able to take a bath but eschewed routine hygiene, then it would be quite easy for me to hate them.

I have always maintained that differences are what makes our country great, what has driven it forward. My only caveat is we should be less of a melting pot and more of a salad bowl of cultures. Lately, though, I cram to understand America. There is NO compromise. It's become a den of vicious Russian kitchen women ready to gut anyone who looks at them sideways. There is a certain irony that America—one of the most diverse nations on earth—can no longer laugh at itself.

Since I'm in education, I couldn't care less about political rap beefs and social hullabaloos. All I ever wanted to do was teach students and all I think they ever wanted to do was learn. Right now, both McGovern and Major Lewis are a threat to my ambition. Thus, they are BOTH enemies to me and I will view them as such. America as it is certainly isn't perfect; but America, after Major Lewis' subterfuge—if he were to be successful—surely wouldn't be either.

I just want to be able to continue to improve on the omelet. Hopefully, McGovern won't be much longer in the courthouse. He has already been in there for over two hours...

Chapter Eleven
with da the rest of da niggas

We weren't happy campers to see McGovern when he finally came from out of the courthouse. It had been almost a three-hour wait. I don't know if you know what it feels like to have an entire town looking at you sideways as if you are Satan's illegitimate stepchild, but that's how the four of us had felt, standing outside all of that time. Every passerby just leered and stared, as though we had committed some terrible crime against their families. What's worse is that when McGovern exited the building, he was accompanied by three White men who were armed with pistols on their hips. Even though their clothing was of this era, it was a little spiffier than most of the townsfolks'. This made me guess they were either law enforcement, business owners, or...

"This gentleman's agreed to put us up for the night," McGovern said, coming up to me, speaking loud enough for the rest of the group to hear.

My eyes darted over toward the men who had followed him. They stood a few feet away, a surprising look of curiosity and nonchalance overriding any other expression. This DEFINITELY told me something was amiss. So far, every White face in the town had looked at us with disdain. These hadn't. Or was I just being paranoid?

Regardless, McGovern's demeanor wasn't giving me a warm, fuzzy vibe either. He appeared more aggressive, suddenly full of hubris. It was almost as if he had transformed into an 11-year-old whose friends had accompanied him to a fight, giving him more confidence. He puffed out his chest, daring anyone to challenge him.

I definitely have something that'll cave your chest in!

The rest of the group glanced over for me to give them a sign. Was it time to act? I didn't know. My gut told me it was, but... So far, McGovern had not done anything overtly wrong except piss us off by making us wait outside for three hours. There was probably a simple explanation for this, though. He could have been trying to find the right people to talk to or from whom to gather information. This would have taken the time and, let's be honest, it's not like McGovern was the brightest lightbulb in the socket.

His innate ignorance aside, he was also displaced in time, which was a learning curve in and of itself. The morals and mores of this society were completely different from those in the present. McGovern probably took time to observe the interaction between others before drumming up the courage to speak with anyone. Yeah, the three hours could easily be justified, but what about these new armed White men who were appearing to stick to us like glue? This could also be easily explained, too.

Despite being a small city, Greenville was still very much a country town surrounded by vast expanses of untamed wilderness. Another thing was that the nation was at war. If I were a White man in this era, I would probably have pistols on me, too. In the end, I couldn't signal to the group to rebel based on a hunch, even though my hunch told me not doing so would come back to bite us in the immediate future. Silently, I looked at the group to signal compliance, then followed McGovern's lead. We were told to get in the back of a wagon. The general and one of the men rode and directed the horses from up front while the other two followed behind on horseback.

Oh, yeah, let me say this before I say anything else.... Riding in the back of a wagon really sucks ASS! On the television and movie screens, it doesn't seem so bad, but trust me, it really is! My booty has never been pounded and bounced around as much as when I was in the back of that damn wagon. It paid for every bump and crook in the ground we traversed. By the time we had traveled five or so miles to our destination, I felt as though I had recently arrived in jail and been violated.

Because it was close to 2100 hours, the night

began to slowly creep in and darken everything. There were lights on in the distance near to a house reminiscent of a small plantation of this era. While it was no mansion à la *Gone with the Wind*, it was breathtaking: A white, two-story, stretched ranch-style house with a long accompanying white wooden fence standing in the distance at the end of a well-worn dirt road. The structure was brightened from the inside by kerosene lamps and a few lit candles.

There appeared to be several slaves, two men and one woman, outside waiting for us as we neared the house.

"Leave yur sacks in the wagun," the man up front with McGovern told us as we came to a stop. "My servants 'll gat 'em."

Again, the group looked over at me to see what our course of action should be. Our weapons were in there. Compliance would leave us defenseless. Yet any insolence could also destroy any backstory the general had presented to the men. Besides, slaves were not supposed to question White men.

I tried to make eye contact with McGovern for some clue. Taking our equipment, is this something he TOLD the man to do, or something the man was simply doing out of courtesy?

Oh. My. God. Who was being the dumbass, now?

As far as this man was concerned, we were ALL slaves. Under normal circumstances, he would not be showing ANY hospitality! And it's not like we could protest leaving our equipment in the wagon. I'm sure Porras and Nguyen were quite adept at fighting in circumstances such as these—Reese, I still didn't know WHAT, if anything, she could do—but regardless of how capable they were, I had to look at the logic of our situation. We were somewhere only God knew, possibly outnumbered by those on the inside. Getting chased by dogs was not in the slightest bit appealing to me.

Additionally, if McGovern WERE in on things—which I surmised he was—he would make an added gun to the three White men's, making a potential skirmish uneven. I didn't even HAVE a gun and Nguyen's, Porras's, and Reese's were tucked neatly away in their rucksacks. No. We would have to be patient and roll the dice by feigning ignorance now, gambling the future would afford us a more favorable position.

I silently indicated compliance once more and we all exited the wagon. Some of us were more grateful than others for finally being let off of that booty-grating monstrosity of a contraption. I don't know if the rest noticed, but I saw the other two White men who had followed us on horseback continuing to quietly study us. At first, I thought this was because they were taken aback by Nguyen's and Porras' ethnic facial characteristics, but this wasn't the case. They stared at us equally, as though we were all some Darwinian experiment. This let me know McGovern had told them SOMETHING, but what? Surely, he wouldn't have been so reckless as to tell them the truth, that we were from the future, on a mission to retrieve some batshit crazy Black man who was hellbent on changing the social structure of the White man in their future? Of course not!

WTF? Then, why ELSE do they keep looking at us that way? Like we're bugs or something?

Climbing out of the front of the wagon, the man who had told us to leave our belongings called out to one of the slaves on the porch.

"Jethro!" he screamed.

Jesus jumped-up Christ! Tell me that slave's name isn't really Jethro? I mean, it's bad enough he has to be a slave, but then he has to suffer a name like Jethro? Man, with slavery the abuses never seemed to stop!

The slave, who had been as stiff as a statute just seconds before, suddenly became animated.

"Yessa, masta! Yessa, masta!" Jethro said, almost falling on the wooden porch, making a fool of himself in an effort to respond to his master's wishes. He quickly recovered and humbly made his way down toward the wagon to grab our things.

"Cletus," the White man commanded to the other slave, ascending the stairs of the porch, "come hare. I ned to spak with you a minute."

You've GOT to be kidding me! Two slaves named Jethro and Cletus? What were the odds?

As McGovern stepped off the wagon, I made my way over towards him, out of earshot of the others.

"What's the play here?" I asked in a soft voice.

"There IS no play," he snarled. "Just do as you're told!"

My eyes blinked several times in rapid succession. I was shocked by the reply and had to replay his words in my mind to see if I had imagined what he had just said.

Hit him in his throat and get it over with.

Slowly, I turned and walked back toward the others, both frustrated and pissed. Reese, noticing my body movements, glanced over at McGovern, and then looked back at me.

"Are things bad?" she whispered.

"Worse," I retorted. "We are in an episode of the *Twilight Zone* and it's not looking too good for the home team. I'm still waiting for Rod Serling to come out to give a macabre monologue."

"What do you want us to do?"

"Sit tight and act as if we don't know what's going on. The more we play dumb, the greater the likelihood we will find out all there is to know about McGovern."

As I was talking to Reese, I noticed how Cletus was interacting with his slave master. Or, rather, how Cletus began to leer at the four of us the longer his slave master talked to him. I was too far away to hear the dialogue, but I developed a discomforting feeling about the slave. Throughout the history of the United States, of the hundreds of slave rebellions that occurred, none had ever truly been successful. The reason? A slave had snitched in virtually every instance!

It was sad to say, but I trusted a slave now even less than I trusted any southern White man. At least with the White man, I knew where I stood. But with a slave? Many would do whatever it took to obtain freedom. And who could blame them? Besides, I would NEVER trust a slave named Cletus.   It sounded like the perfect moniker for an Uncle Tom.

After the slave master had finished talking to him, he brought Cletus over to us.

"Yur slave masta will be insad fur the nat," he said, addressing the rest of the group rather roughly through me. "You two niggars and whateva dose two ur will sleep with da rest of da niggars in da back. Cletus 'll take you dere."

I could feel Reese's arm now twitching in earnest. The N-word was in full effect. We became oblivious to McGovern and what he was doing. With Jethro busy grabbing our things from the wagon, we reluctantly followed Cletus to the area back of the house and into what seemed to be a jungle of untamed vegetation and trees. The further away from the house we got, the more the night and darkness embraced us.

After walking for a few minutes seemingly nowhere and tripping over a log she didn't see, Reese let out, "Where on earth are we going?"

"Ware da rest of da niggas are," Cletus said matter-of-factly. We were soon brought to a clearing. While it was hard to make out, flickers of light could be seen inside some of the shotgun shacks we suddenly came upon. While the others may not have realized it, I instantly knew what this smattering of shanty houses was: Slave quarters. And they were EXACTLY how I pictured them to be: Spartan, practically bare, reminding me of something straight out of the Stone Age, minus the antiquated stoves inside. Cletus brought us to what appeared to be two empty cabins right next to one another.

Reese whispered, "I'm not going to even ask where the bathrooms are, but I really do have to use one."

"Good," I replied, "because I don't think you'll like the answer."

"Two of yalls can slept in dere," Cletus pointed to one cabin before pointing to the other, "and two can slept in dere."

Looking at the cabins from the outside, they BOTH looked equally raggedy and dilapidated. Grabbing onto the door, Reese was surprised to find no doorknob.

"If there are no locks on the doors," she asked incredulously, "how do you secure them?"

Cletus looked at her as if she had lost her mind. "Whatcha need a lack fur? I ain't gat nuthin' to hide and masta don't lack slaves who have sumthin' ta hide."

Slavery, you gotta love it: Brainwashing at its best!

Reese took one peek inside and hastily closed the door. "Oh, hell, no!" she exclaimed in protest to the conditions she saw. "I'd rather sleep outside."

Not fully understanding her reaction, Cletus responded, "Whut's the matta? You see a rat? I can kill 'em for yur ifn you want me to."

I grabbed Reese and shoved her into the cabin. I put my body on the closed door to prevent her from running out. Luckily, she took the hint.

"That's okay, Cletus. I'll kill the rat. She'll be okay."

I addressed Nguyen and Porras. "Rest up. I have a feeling we're going to have a looong day ahead of us tomorrow."

"We do, too," they chimed together.

Turning to go into his cabin, Nguyen laughed, replying, "And good luck with killing that rat!"

For some reason, Cletus stared at me weirdly for a few moments before finally turning to walk away.

As I closed the door, Reese made her way over to the stove in an attempt to light it. I don't think she realized she had left her lighter in her rucksack until she actually touched an old piece of wood sitting at the bottom of the stove. She sighed with a defiant tone. Luckily for us, the inside of the cabin was not all dark. It seemed to be situated at the perfect angle to be bathed in the full radiance of the moonlight, such as it were.

"I wasn't kidding when I told you earlier that I had to go to the bathroom," Reese said in frustration.

Like a kid, I asked, "Do you have to do number one or number two?"

"What do YOU think? I did number one a couple of times in the bushes on our trek toward Greenville, remember?"

I remember laughing because you were scared to drop your trousers and squat, thinking you were going to get bit on the butt by a mosquito.

"Yes, I remember," I replied. "Well, I know it's rather primitive, but you're in the military and I'm sure you've had to go do number two in the woods at some point in time."

"True," she acknowledged, "but I've always had the courtesy of having toilet paper. We left everything, even our bare essentials, in the sacks. I don't HAVE any right now."

"Well, you can always use leaves and grass to clean yourself."

Reese took that statement as me trying to be funny. I wasn't. I was trying to be practical.

"You know," she retorted, "right now I'm inclined to pull this hunk of wood from out of this stove and hit you upside the head with it. But first, I'm going to go use the bathroom. I suddenly remembered I have some wet wipes stashed away in my pockets. I'll just have to make them work."

As she was leaving out the door, I sarcastically commented, "Be sure to watch out for the wolves!"

Reese rolled her eyes at me and slammed the door. A few moments later, I felt compelled to check and see what direction she had gone. As my eyes adjusted to the darkness and struggled to fine-tune images, a shadowy figure in the distance came into view. It was someone hiding behind a tree, watching our cabin, but I didn't fixate on the person, I didn't want him to know I had seen him. After a few seconds, I went back inside and sat down on the dirt floor next to the stove.

Why would Cletus be spying on us? My intuition about him was still working overtime. Was he a pervert, wanting to get a peek at Cantaloupe booty as she took a squat to use the restroom? Or was he his slave master's spy? If so, this would also make him McGovern's lackey.

Chapter Twelve
the truth about mcgovern

Despite our current lodging, I had managed to become quite comfortable. This was attributable to our weariness and the drain of the day more than anything else. Walking with seemingly no end in sight, then sitting outside waiting another couple of hours, took a bite out of me. Luckily the shotgun shack Reese and I were in had two beds, if that word could be used, near one another. For all intents and purposes, we were expected to sleep in a wooden box filled with straw. There were no mattresses or sheets. The pillows were only rudimentary semblances of full loose cotton.

I didn't really care much about the awful sleeping arrangements. I was so fatigued I could have fallen asleep on the top of a hot tin roof during a summer thunderstorm. After her adventure using the bathroom, Reese came back into the cabin and found me stretched out laying on one of the beds.

Upon closer inspection of where she was expected to sleep, she noticed the straw and said, "Oh, HELL no! I am NOT sleeping in…. Who even does that?"

"Slaves, Reese," I said, tired of her complaining. "That's who sleeps in something like this. Why do you keep acting as if you're expecting the *Love Boat*? What part of slavery and 1862 do you not get? After being placed with the rest of da niggas in the back, reality should have set in."

I thought she would react negatively to my rhetoric. Instead, it seemed to cause Reese to realize she was being a bit extra. She took a moment to dial down her demeanor. At the same time, I realized I had been a bit extra with my last statement. Consider Reese's perspective. Her fiancé had disappeared without a trace and she later became ensnared in his deadly machinations. None of this was her fault. She was only trying to find answers. Reese was simply like the rest of our group of color: Just trying to make it. Except, she probably felt the added burden of guilt because of her ties to Major Lewis. He was, after all, the reason for our current adventure.

"I don't know, Dr. Mazique," she said, "all of this seems so…surreal. I mean, you learn about slavery in school—or at least what they allow you to—and you KNOW it happened…you KNOW it existed, but to actually see it up close and personal is unsettling. Besides the whips and chains, it's stuff like this— sleeping in a box full of straw for a bed—that our people had to endure. It's like a myriad of microaggressions and demeaning acts all piled on top of overtly inhumane treatment."

I attempted to lighten the mood. "You mean, like having to live with names like Jethro and Cletus?"

"That seems to be the least of Black people's problems right now."

"And what do you think ours currently are?"

"McGovern."

I confirmed her assessment. "Agreed, but first we have to find your fiancé."

"Something tells me we won't have to look far."

"Are you still getting the feeling he's following us?"

Shaking her head and finally giving in to the exhaustion of the day, Reese plopped down into her bed of straw.

"No, more like he's already here."

I laughed. "You two share some sort of psychic bond or something?"

"I don't need to be psychic. I just know my man."

"Every woman claims to know their man," I protested. "That doesn't mean they actually do."

It was Reese's turn to laugh. "Most women DO know their man. You guys aren't that hard to figure out. The thing is, I don't pretend to exist in a bubble. Knowing your man is about embracing him—warts and all—and not being Jedi-mind-tricked by the good times or by the intimacy."

"So...what are Major Lewis' warts?"

Reese took a few seconds to consider before replying, "His passion. It's his gift AND his curse. He's programmed to succeed, sometimes at any cost.

"There's another thing you should also know. These shenanigans might make Major Lewis look like a radical who hates White people and America, but that's far from the truth. He loves America, but he loves Black people more. If he had to make a choice between the two..."

"He wouldn't hesitate to make it in favor of Black people," I retorted, interrupting Reese, completing her sentence for her. "I understand that, but this also beggars the question. What pushed him to the point of planning all of this? What made him think he had no other choice? That is the million-dollar question."

Reese decided to switch gears. "But, can I ask YOU something?"

"Go ahead."

"Why did you really agree to come on this mission? I mean, with all of your knowledge about history and everything Blacks went through, isn't there SOME part of you who wishes Major Lewis is successful?"

I began to smile. "I would be lying if I told you no. However, I don't believe in quick fixes or easy solutions. They usually lead to disaster. Yes, America has a lot of problems, but it's a great country with a great future if we work together as a people. We can't allow Major Lewis to succeed. The possible chaos resulting from doing so might doom the entire world."

"Or, it could make it a BETTER world," Reese cut in.

"Maybe. Yet the other reason I'm on this mission is because your fiancé played me like a fiddle. And he did it all the while playing to my arrogance and ego. His countless questions about some of the most controversial historical figures in U.S. history now make sense. There was definitely a method to his madness. But I abhor anyone playing me, especially for a dastardly plot such as this. I felt that since I helped to create a monster, I was obligated to help destroy it.

"The last reason I agreed to come is because I'm a historian. Mentioning "time machine" to me is sort of like waving a piece of crack in front of a drug fiend. What did you expect me to do? NOT come along? Notwithstanding the Major Lewis issue, I would have risked life and limb to go back in the past regardless. I don't believe any historian worth his or her salt could have turned down such an opportunity."

Reese snickered a little at the "crack fiend" reference, but now it was time for her to come clean.

"Where is your head at, Reese, with all of this, and what is going on? Do YOU want your fiancé to be successful? And if it comes down to it, are we going to be able to depend on you to go against him if that's what it takes?"

She was too slow to respond, so I answered for her.

"Fine. I get it. You love him. He's your man and you won't directly move against him. I can't hold that against you, and I don't think Nguyen and Porras will either. But if that IS the case, don't interfere with us if and when we have to deal with your fiancé. Okay?"

It took Reese a few seconds, but she finally responded with, "Deal."

After that, we both closed our eyes and almost immediately let the straw and exhaustion from the day take us to sleep.

***

Do you know how it feels to be sound asleep, only to be abruptly awoken by the touch of cold, hard, sharp steel pressed firmly against your throat? Here's a hint: It doesn't produce a warm, fuzzy feeling. But it did wake me up out of a deep slumber. I will also admit the straw bed felt a little better than it was supposed to. Or did it feel comfortable because I was just THAT tired?

I really wanted to examine the question further, but I had to concentrate on the knife which, felt as if it were about to cut my skin and leave a nasty scar.

A hand was placed over my mouth. A male voice said, "Stay quiet and come with me. I don't want to kill you, but if you make any noise or draw attention to us, I won't hesitate. You'll be dead before you can say, 'Ali Baba and the Forty thieves."

While I get the hint, that was really a stupid thing to say.

I nodded acceptance and the hand was removed from my face. As I got out of bed, the knife was moved toward my lower back, against my spine. I looked over for Reese, but she was nowhere to be found in her box of straw. Figures, he would have woken her up first before awakening me. Stealthily, we exited the cabin and made our way through the woods, away from the other slave cabins. Since my assailant was walking behind me with the knife to my back, guiding me, I didn't see his face, but I didn't need to; I knew with whom I was dealing.

After about five minutes of walking, I saw Reese, who, by the looks of her body language, had been impatiently waiting for us. Instead of having an aura of joy from a warm reunion, her face had the look of a rabid dog about to snap. Even Ray Charles couldn't have missed her fury, it was THAT obvious. According to McGovern, Major Lewis was one of the most dangerous men on the planet. Yet at that moment, I'm quite sure even he was reluctant to face a pissed-off Reese.

I walked over to her and turned around to face the man of the hour. I told Major Lewis, "I was wondering when you would show up."

"While I would say it is a surprise seeing you in 1862, Doctor," he confidently replied, "I figured the military would at least reach out to you regarding background information about me."

He was smug and I couldn't stand it. I looked him over as he stood in front of us in army fatigues and camouflage. Interestingly enough, he had no visible firearm on him, only an archaic wooden bow affixed to his back with multiple arrows in a crude leather quiver. His face was unshaven and the hair on his head was somewhat matted. All in all, Major Lewis looked quite well for a man who technically would not be born for over a century and a half from now.

Reese, silent since I had stood next to her, had the look of pisstivity. While we were both eager to have a shot at Major Lewis to extract our own personal pound of flesh, she beat me to the punch. She was also more direct than I ever would have been.

"What the fuck is going on, Darryl?" Reese demanded to know. "And what have you dragged me into?"

He smiled. "Well, it's nice to see you too, honey."

"I'm NOT in the mood!"

"Okay, then. I'll get right to it. But full disclosure, some of this is going to shock even you. I have several jobs within the military. However, if I get called in to investigate or rectify something, it is NEVER a good thing. And sometimes what I do takes years to uncover.

"Just to give you an idea of HOW bad this situation is, on a scale of one to 10, with one already starting off as bad, this is FUBAR."

"I heard Nguyen and Porras using that word earlier. What does it mean?"

"It's an acronym for Fucked Up Beyond All Recognition, the point we are now at, which is BEYOND a 10. I know it might look like I took extreme measures by going back in time unauthorized, but believe me, I had no other choice."

Rolling her eyes and crossing her arms, Reese let out, "I'm STILL waiting with bated breath for you to explain."

"Okay, dear, here it is. About eight years ago, we got a ping about White extremism in the military. And when I say 'we', I mean the government agency with three letters that I actually work for."

"You mean you're not really a part of the military?" I questioned.

"No. That's just my cover."

Reese looked taken aback. *I guess she didn't know her man as well as she THOUGHT she did, huh?*

"At the midpoint of Obama's presidency, there was a surge of the far-right, conservative movement on many different levels. This drew our attention to several key people within McGovern's inner circle. At that time, he wasn't even on our radar, nor had he obtained the rank of general.

"But the people around him were all affiliated with the Timestream project. That's when I first became aware the military had such capability, or at least that it had built a working time machine. By coincidence, it was also around this period, Dr. Mazique, that you published your paper, *Return to Nubia*. I think you can now understand why I began to take an interest in your work. At first, it was only a curiosity related to my probe within the Chronal Spatial department.

"By the time Trump was about to leave office, extremism in the military had worsened and my probe had gotten deeper. You know how you and everyone else think the January sixth riot on the Capitol building was just an unorganized cluster with disillusioned Trump supporters? That wasn't the case. McGovern and several other high-ranking military personnel had planned a coup by raiding the building, kidnapping, and then executing prominent legislators and key congressional officials whom they deemed a threat to their overall plans."

The fantasy being spun seemed too incredulous to me. "I don't believe you," I said. "That would be far too complex for someone like Trump to plan."

"Trump had nothing to do with it," Major Lewis replied. "No one with half a brain would leave it up to that moron to plan anything. He would have bragged about it on Twitter!

"No, what was done behind the scenes was done without Trump's knowledge. Didn't you ever wonder why 20% of the people prosecuted by the FBI for their participation of the day were current or former military veterans? It wasn't too hard to organize: AI was unleashed on social media to sow discord. The yahoos and conspiracy theorists did the rest."

Reese finally joined the conversation. "If that were the case, if McGovern and others were behind it, why did January sixth end badly? The mob didn't come close to a coup. It was more like gas exchanged after eating bad food. All they did was smash some windows, sit in some office chairs, and walk around pouting!"

"January sixth ended badly because McGovern called off the coup at the last minute. With no organized plan—no one to provide resources or direction—it simply fell apart."

I wondered. "Why did McGovern call off the coup?"

"Because about a week earlier, December 30th to be exact, the Chronal Spatial department made a breakthrough. It finally succeeded in sending an inanimate object through to the future. McGovern knew it was only a matter of time before the scientists would be able to replicate sending an inanimate object back through to the past, and at some point after that humans would be able to enter the portal.

"Why engineer a coup that may or may not succeed when you can manipulate the timestream? Every important piece of legislation this nation has ever passed could be changed simply by going back in time. And that's just the beginning of the possibilities. Do you want to make sure a particular president never got elected? Go back and erase the beginning of his timeline to ensure he never existed in the first place."

Now I felt like a kid begging for answers. "Are you saying that's what McGovern planned on doing?"

"Before I reply, answer THIS question, Dr. Mazique. Are you familiar with Major James R. Crowe?"

I had to calm myself down to think; the conversation had my adrenaline flowing! I was familiar with the name but couldn't place the rhythm or reason. Finally, after a couple of seconds, I stated, "I don't remember who that is."

"With all you have going on right now, I'm sure you don't. That's why I'm going to remind you. There were originally six founding members of the Klan: J. Calvin Jones, John B. Kennedy, John C. Lester, Frank McCord, and…"

"And Major James R. Crowe," I said, completing Major Lewis' sentence.

Now, I remembered who he was.

Much like Nathan Bedford Forrest, he had disavowed himself of the Klan during his later years. Still, what was his connection to…?

"General McGovern is a direct descendant of Major Crowe, on his mother's side."

Though my jaw began to drop to the floor from the revelation, for some reason I found myself coming to McGovern's defense. "But that doesn't mean he…"

"McGovern is a Grand Wizard in the Klan, its top member in an affiliated organization. There was no way normal military security measures would have discovered this. His background was a craftily held secret and he was groomed from birth to be a part of the military, to make the right connections, say the right things, and rise in rank. He's also careful not to use too much technology. This is the reason why, despite being a general, he's kind of an idiot around computers. They leave footprints that can't be erased. He has always preferred the typewriter."

"This doesn't make sense," I protested. "If Crowe himself was resentful of what the Klan eventually became, why would any of his descendants think differently?"

"Because part of his family never forgave him for reneging on what Bedford and he had started. They believed Crowe was a coward for abandoning his convictions.

"In their eyes, he had nothing to be ashamed of and shouldn't have regretted establishing the Klan. They have looked for recompense ever since. McGovern grew up with that frame of reference."

"I assume you have evidence to back all of this up?" I asked.

Major Lewis assertively responded, "Yes, I do: Wiretaps, recordings, paperwork, and hard drives. I basically have enough to put McGovern and his underlings in jail for quite a while, if not outright killed by a firing squad. Believe me, though, this thing is bigger than any of you realize. It goes above McGovern. He's just the largest fish I've been able to gather evidence on."

I could tell Reese was being swayed by Major Lewis' words. This was understandable. She was in love with him and just needed a somewhat reasonable explanation to assuage her anger. I, on the other hand, demanded more clarification as to his actions.

"What you have told us," I slowly started saying, "explains a lot. But what it DOESN'T explain is you going rogue and entering the time portal to alter the past. Surely, there was someone you could have reached out to regarding McGovern? Regardless, you're no better than he. You've been planning this for years.

"It's the reason you sought me out and took my

classes. It's also the reason you pumped me for information seemingly about every important historical figure of the 18th and 19th centuries!"

Major Lewis didn't deny the accusations. Shrugging his shoulders, he replied, "Yeah. So what?"

"What do you mean, so what? You played me!"

"Part of what I do for a living, Dr. Mazique, is kill people and help to topple governments, and you want me to feel bad for manipulating you? Good luck with that. I did what I HAD to do. Before McGovern, I never thought time travel was possible. And now that I do know it's possible, it's come down to this."

"It's come down to what?" I crammed to understand.

"Dr. Mazique, as much as you try to stay in the middle, you can't on this. You see what's going on in America: The divisiveness, the anger between races, and the building of White nationalism. This goes beyond your omelet. What good is it to eat breakfast when you're erased from history?"

"You sound like a paranoid man gone mad," I told him.

"And you sound like one of the house slaves who is about to tell the slave master his niggas in da back are about to rebel."

When I was younger, any man who had made a

statement like that would have immediately received a crisp overhand right to his jaw. But I was no longer young and foolish.

I STILL wanted to beat his ass, though.

Perhaps a fight between us would come later, but right now Major Lewis needed to know where I stood.

Beat his ass! Beat his ass!

"I get so TIRED of Black people who claim someone is an Uncle Tom simply because they disagree with them. It's irresponsible and foolish. This isn't some George Clinton song, where we are all *One Nation Under a Groove*, living under one homogeneous thought! The Black nation is large enough to have a plethora of perspectives, and mine is this: What you are doing is wrong and goes against nature and God. If you tamper with time, you play with fire. We don't know WHAT the possible adverse reverberations will be!"

"So, we simply let McGovern and his minions off the hook?"

"No, of course not! We take him back to the present and turn him over to the proper authorities."

Major Lewis stared at me. "You know, you really are naive," he said.

"Maybe. But I know what it is to be consumed with anger and hate. It can make you delusional, and I will take naivete over delusion anytime. Naivete doesn't cause the destruction of mankind."

"No, just the destruction of the Black race."

We both paused for a few seconds and the moment of silence, though fleeting, felt suffocating. There was still much to be said, debates to be had, and it was too early in the morning for tempers to be running this high. We had both said much for each other to consider. Perhaps this is why Major Lewis offered me an olive branch of sorts.

"As it is right now," he finally stated, "both of us seem pretty stuck on our beliefs. How about I give you a day to consider? That will also give you time to talk to Nguyen and Porras. I will come back tomorrow night at about the same time. You can let me know what you want to do about McGovern and where all of you stand on me changing the past. Deal?"

"Deal," I agreed, looking over at Reese, who once more had become mute. Major Lewis attempted to grab her hand. She slowly pulled away from him and began gazing at the ground to avoid eye contact.

"Just go, Darryl," she said in a soft, low voice. "Just go. I will see you tomorrow night."

He hesitated, and in his hesitation, I felt their mutual pain.

Major Lewis thought Reese would be more

understanding of his antics, while Reese probably thought he would be more grounded in reality. They had both been wrong. Saying nothing more, he eventually walked away and disappeared into the night.

Chapter Thirteen
my judas moment

After Major Lewis and I had our rhetorical tête-à-tête, I fell asleep thinking about our exchange. I realize now he had been holding back during our infrequent debates after class. And Reese had been right in her description of his warts; he was quite passionate about his beliefs. Almost TOO passionate. But were his actions wrong? I remembered Major Lewis' words and had to reconsider.

Just how deep did this rabbit hole go and who else was involved? If McGovern, a brigadier general, was in the mix, was there anyone of a higher rank in this conspiracy? Plus, Major Lewis WAS right. There was a growing divide between Blacks and Whites in the country, between the have-nots and the haves, the disenfranchised and the one percent. Was Major Lewis really paranoid, or was he paranoid like a fox?

If I ran the numbers in my head, history gave credence to his claims. America WAS due for some major conflict in the immediate future. Consider the major wars in which the United States has been involved and the growing global destruction of the conflicts as it's moved into the modern era.

The ***Revolutionary War***, 1775 - 1783; the ***War of 1812***, 1812 - 1815; the ***Second Seminole War***,

1835 - 1842; the *Mexican American War*, 1846 - 1848; the *American Civil War*, 1861 - 1865; *World War I*, 1914 - 1918, *World War II*, 1939 - 1945; the *Korean War*, 1950 - 1953; the **Vietnam War**, 1955 - 1975; the **Gulf War**, 1990 - 1991; the **U.S. War in Afghanistan**, 2001- 2021.

Now, take some of its darkest social, political, and economic highlights: Slavery, women's suffrage, *Plessy versus Ferguson*, the *Spanish Flu*, the *Red Summer of 1919*, the *Tulsa Race Massacre*, the *Tuskegee Syphilis Experiment*, the *Great Depression*, *Operation Wetback*, the Civil Rights unrest of the 1960s, *Watergate*, the *Vietnam War* protests of the 1970s, the *Oil Embargo*, the *Iran Hostage Crisis*, the *HIV Epidemic* of the 1980s, the *Crack Epidemic* of the 1980s, the *Savings and Loans Crisis*, the *Enron Scandal*, the terrorist attack of September 11, 2001, the *Great Recession*, the *Covid-19 Epidemic/Experiment*, the rising gun violence in schools, the dispute of presidential election results, and the storming of the nation's capital by a mob with all of the intellectual capacity of a doorknob.

Sure. I know some smartass somewhere is going to mention a myriad of things I missed, but I think lay people understand what I'm trying to say.

My point with all of the above is that things seem

to be getting crazier and more intense. History indicates America is ripe for some major adversity, a fair comeuppance for its past actions. I mean, it DID steal a country from one race and then kidnap another to build its empire. Throughout the centuries, America has attempted to bully and assert its own moral code on the world.

The problem with this last part is that it's kind of like a $20 Prospect Avenue professional woman of the night attempting to tell everyone else how to lead their lives. It is both hypocritical and contradictory.

Who could blame Major Lewis for wanting to give Blacks a win? Was the first O.J. Simpson verdict supposed to be the ONLY bone thrown at Black people?

Come on, now. All of you know. O.J. Simpson. Really. Was. Guilty!

If social or civil unrest in the United States between people of color and Whites was inevitable, could I blame Major Lewis for wanting to be proactive and strike first? No...but that doesn't necessarily make him right.

Okay. I'll bite. I'll take the other side and convince you.

If Major Lewis is allowed to change time, he could destroy all of mankind.

Have you looked at the world lately? It's not like we'd lose much! Everyone is at each other's throats.

China is flexing its muscles. Little Kim Jung Ung is still walking around like a North Korean Gary Coleman, itching to pick a fight. People are battling and dying in Africa, and I won't even mention Haiti. Russia is attacking Ukraine...and getting its butt kicked. Diseases are being created in labs. Then the public has to wear masks until all of the pharmaceutical companies who are helping to spew misinformation become economically bloated from the fallout. Could things really get ANY worse?

But what if they do?

So what? You have the chronal displacement doohickey attached to your arm. Whatever happens, it won't affect you!

But I'm the one who helped Major Lewis with his plan.

Boo-hoo. Daaayumn, get over yourself! Who are you supposed to be? The messiah of the Black race? Its savior? There was only ONE Jesus and you don't have locks like him. Have you ever considered Major Lewis as the person who is right and you're the one who is wrong?

No.

Well, maybe you should. And perhaps you should also consider his analogy about you being the nigga who betrays the rest of the slaves for the slave master.

For one, you know I abhor that word. And for another, that's absurd! I'm no one's Uncle Tom.

Really? You know as well as I do that many of those slaves who betrayed their brethren did so because they were scared; they were scared of the changes that came with being free, so it was easier to turn on their own and remain where they were. This begs the question: Are you afraid of the change that might come if Black people are finally, truly free and equal?

I know you're probably waiting for me to pause or hesitate so you can sow more doubt, but I have never been more resolved. I'm not afraid of Black people finally being free. We've ALWAYS been free. Even in slavery, they couldn't break us because of a certain rhythm dancing in our souls. We weathered the storm and outlasted our enemies.

Black people are the first, the true kings and queens of the world. We STILL have people trying to figure out how we did the pyramids. But we are an honorable people—a spiritual people—and there is no honor in obtaining our freedom at the cost of others. No matter WHAT we have gone through or are currently going through, I won't be deterred from MY beliefs.

Come on, man. They put Bill Cosby AND R. Kelly in jail!

Really? Is that what we're doing now?

Well, I was running out of material. The Trump jokes only go so far!

So, are we through? Because, I have spoken. There IS nothing else to say.

Oooh! You sound sooo authoritative! Yes. For the record, I knew you wouldn't change your mind. I just had to test you to make sure you stayed strong.

Yeah, sure.

I'm SERIOUS! What sort of an anger translator would I be if I turned you against your convictions? It's one of the reasons I enjoy hanging out with you.

You mean, even though you're actually a part of my subconscious and are stuck with me?

Okay, you busted me. But since we're having this intimate discussion...what are you going to do about McGovern and Major Lewis? I know you feel what I feel coming. Are you prepared to do what you need to do?

I've been thinking about it, and while I don't relish the idea, I won't run from it, either. I know what I need to do if it comes to that. I won't hesitate with EITHER party.

Are you SURE? It's going to require you to regress to that part you've covered up over the years. Sometimes, men only show respect or surrender when they...

Realize a force equal to or greater than themselves. I remember...I remember.

Can you be that force again?

Yes.

Are you sure?

Yes.

You had better be, because...here they...come...

***

I almost jumped out of the straw bed as my eyes crept open from a deep, brief slumber and found Cletus standing over me.

"What the hell?" I grunted, half from anger and half from the exhaustion of sleep.

"Time ta gat up."

I quickly looked out of what were supposed to be the cabin's windows. On the horizon, the sun was only beginning to flirt with the darkness of the night.

"What time is it?" I asked in protest, looking over at Reese who was loudly snoring, still asleep.

Whenever we get back to the present, she now has TWO nicknames: Cantaloupe booty and Foghorn.

"Masta lack his niggas up eerily. He say a eerily nigga is a prodack...is a prodict..."

"Productive," I said, helping Cletus along.

"Yeah. He say, an eerily nigga is a productive nigga. And I am to be productive."

You NEED to aim to pronounce and enunciate your words better, fool.

"Besads, ya'll might nut be sleepy ifn' ya wouldn't have been in da woods lat last night."

I attempted to play coy, to throw Cletus off. Had he followed us into the woods with Major Lewis?

"What are you talking about?"

"Ifn' dat's how ya want to play thangs. But just so ya know? Dat dog don't hunt 'round here."

Looks like Cletus told you he knows you're lying. And if he knows about Major Lewis or THINKS he has something to tell his master, we could all be in trouble. Well, Dr. Mazique, you have another name to add to your list. I sure hope you have the gonads to do what it takes when it comes down to it. I hope you are ready.

Chapter Fourteen
reese's breakfast experience

For me, the day was one of discovery and verification of what I had studied throughout the decades: How did slaves actually live? What did they eat? What chores were they assigned? How hard was the actual work? Was it the exaggerated stuff of legends or was it truly the back-breaking drudgery movies like *Roots* made it out to be?

Because my parents had been from the South and I had spent time down there, I had some insights, particularly when it came to work. The way both sides of my family labored had always amazed me. My uncles could work outside in the hot Arkansas sun all day with a smile on their faces, never seeming to tire, and my aunties would be out there with them, too, just as productive. Being young and foolish, I thought I could work the way they did. Once, when I spent the summer in Pine Bluff, I asked to go out to the fields in the country with them. I thought it would be fun.

You might walk over here, but you're going to be limping back.

It was anything BUT fun. They rode me harder than Seabiscuit, or at least it felt that way. I tried to keep up with my uncles, but they moved like steroid-fueled madmen, throwing bales of hay, milking cows, and then picking cotton.

Yes, even in the late '70s, there were still people who picked cotton by hand.

That's another thing. Picking cotton isn't sexy. While a cotton boll doesn't have thorns, it does have dried bristles that are often sharp and can cut. If you're not wearing gloves or you don't know what you're doing, your hands will definitely bleed.

Everyone must have thought I was prissy, the way I picked cotton. I was slow and deliberate and simply couldn't keep up with my relatives. I didn't even try, and why should I have? My uncles picked so much cotton so fast, their collective nickname was *The Cotton Gin*. I was even told my mother could pick 70 pounds of cotton by the time she was four years old.

Good for them! They should have been booked on **The View**. *But I wonder. If the women had called them cotton pickers, would that have been a racist or politically incorrect thing to say, even though that's what they were? Oh, the conundrums of today's society!*

By noon, I was crying and begging to escape from work, back to Pine Bluff, to my grandmother's house. With disdain, my uncles labeled me lazy and trifling—said I was too much a city boy—and begrudgingly drove me back to shut me up. This was my experience working in the South.

Later, once I learned about the horrors of

slavery, I knew the history of the work associated with it was no exaggeration. My uncles and aunties worked the way they did because it was in their bones and in their blood. This dedication to work had been passed down through the ages. It was how their descendants had lived, when many of them had to work infinitely harder under a whip.

Because of this, I sort of knew how our day was going to transpire. We would be expected to labor in some sort of capacity, even if we were guests. We were still supposedly McGovern's slaves and would be looked at sideways if we didn't do the work of slaves. Regardless, I was excited to explore and do research.

Nguyen, Porras, and Reese did not seem to share my enthusiasm. They didn't know what to expect, nor did they see what was coming. Since they had done manual labor in some sort of capacity for the military, they thought they could handle whatever was thrown their way. What was that slogan the army used to have?

We do more before 9AM than most people do all day. Well, I bet your asses have NEVER worked harder than a slave!

They were going to find out slaves did more in one day than most people did all week. And working so hard didn't exactly ensure slaves to a long life. In fact, even by 1850, the average life expectancy of a slave was only 21.4 years of age, while the average life expectancy of someone White was 40 years. Slave life in the Antebellum South, though, was considerably longer than those who lived in colonial America.

In that age, White people essentially worked the dog doo-doo out of Black people!

Africans put to work during colonial America only lasted an average of seven years; the work was THAT hard! In some other countries—like on the sugar plantations in Brazil and Haiti—it was invariably worse. Although slavery was brutal in the United States, the reason why the population of African Americans is so high today is because they were the only Africans during chattel slavery who lived long enough to reproduce. In the other regions where Africans were displaced during the diaspora, slaves didn't live long enough to copulate, so the enslaved population could be increased through natural births.

You mean, even Cialis or Viagra wouldn't have helped? I guess when you are dead, horniness doesn't matter!

While I tried focusing on doing historical research, I was often distracted by Reese who seemed to have a comment for everything. Strangely, though, at some point her complaints went from being irritating to amusing. She thought beforehand she knew about slavery but found out she didn't know it as well as she thought she had. In watching her verbally flail about, Reese also gave me an idea for my next book, although I doubted my snooty academic publishers would let me go with the title I wanted to use. It was too inflammatory: **How to Be a Prodactive, Eerily Nigga 101**.

I must be rubbing off on you.

Yes, and I have to admit that is somewhat disturbing.

At any rate, I want to give the book this name to mirror the times it represents. It would be a historical account of how slaves operated daily and what was expected of them from the slave master. Most people—even many African Americans—don't think about actual slave culture when they think about slavocracy in the Antebellum South. They know about the whips and the chains—yes, the macroaggressions—but what about the microaggressions? The things like the straw in the beds and the bare earth cabin floor? With such a book, Reese and the others might not have been taken by surprise, not that everyone is going to travel back in the past to 1862.

But it is my job as a history professor to teach and to spread the knowledge in a way my students can understand. In education, we call this being student-centric.

I don't think anyone who's following this tale wants to hear all of that pedagogical crap. Big deal, you have a doctorate. This isn't about you. Stop puffing out your chest and get back to the story!

Point taken.

I began observing Reese during the day as much as I did any of the slaves around me. I was sure she had been a comedian in a previous life. The first devilments began early in the morning. Most of the slaves ate what was called breakfast in their tiny shacks. Since we were guests and were without food, Cletus brought all of us to a cabin whose sole inhabitant was an older slave named Shirley. She didn't say much and only motioned to usher us inside when we arrived. Shirley had evidently been told to provide us with a meal. Crude plates and forks were given to us before she went around slopping food on our plates from out of two old and blackened cast iron skillets. We were given cornbread and pork to eat. While Nguyen and Porras consumed their food like a pair of savages— *I guess they were REALLY hungry*—Reese just looked oddly at what she was given.

She poked at the pork as though she were checking to make sure it wouldn't jump up from her plate. I began eating and looked over at her.

"What's wrong?" I queried in a low voice.

"I KNOW they don't expect me to eat this...for breakfast?" was her response.

"Actually, I'm surprised we're even getting this."

"Why do you say that? It's not like this is top sirloin."

"Because most slaves didn't have access to meat like this, particularly in the morning. If they were given parts of the pig, it was usually the parts most people didn't eat, like the intestines, which we call chitterlings today. Be lucky this isn't cornmeal and molasses. Protein was usually a delicacy."

Reese glanced at her food pitifully. "Well, I might have to skip THIS delicacy because, number one, even the cornbread doesn't look appetizing; and, number two, I can't eat this heavy this early in the morning."

I hate to tell you this, Cantaloupe booty, but your ass is going to starve!

By now, Nguyen and Porras had finished eating and were angling Shirley for more food. Reluctantly, she obliged. She thought they were greedy, especially for guests.

"Reese, I wouldn't advise skipping this meal. For one, we don't know if we're going to get another; and, number two, I don't think you realize how hard you are going to have to work today and how long you are going to work."

"What is THAT supposed to mean?"

It means a hard head makes a soft behind!

"Okay. Let me break this down. In THIS reality, you are a SLAVE. In this reality, slaves often work an average of 14 to 16 hours a day in decent weather. On sugar plantations, it was sometimes 18 hours a day. During inclement weather is the only time you MIGHT only work eight to 10 hours. And slaves worked that way six days a week. The only time they had off was usually on Sunday. Remember, you are property. Damn your feelings or your work conditions. There is no such thing as Human Resources or maintaining a positive workplace environment.

"Since this is early spring in Tennessee and the weather is fine, there is a reason why Cletus got us up before the sun rose. We are expected to be productive, early niggas who will work from sun up—which is about 0600 hours—to sundown, which is about 2000 hours. This would be close to 14 hours of work. Now, IF we get something else to eat during the day..."

Reese interrupted me. "What do you mean, IF we get something else to eat? Of course, they're going to feed us something else! Slavery be damned, how can someone expect a person to work hard for that long if they don't feed them more than once?"

I replied sarcastically. "Because you are a SLAVE."

Reese became pissed off and didn't know what else to say, so she resorted to childlike behavior. "I'm NOT a slave. Your MOMMA'S a slave!"

I continued to snicker, which only pissed her off

more. "Maybe so, but at least my momma would be smart enough to eat the food given to her. While I figure this place is big and profitable enough to ensure its workforce gets fed more than once, one can never be sure."

By this time, Cletus, being nosy and noticing Reese wasn't eating, came over. He pointed at her.

"Whut da matta whit cha? Sum thang wrong whit da food? Or is ya jus an uppity nigga?"

Reese's arm began to twitch. "Did this country bumpkin just call me an uppity nigga?" she asked underneath her breath.

More loudly, she said, "You, the man who needs *Hooked on Phonics*, has the NERVE to talk about me?

Fight! Fight! Fight! Steal on his ass, Reese! Knock him into next week!

I tried to intervene. "It's not that she's uppity, Cletus, we're just used to a different type of food."

"Ma be so," Cletus retorted, "but you'n the other men's folk seems ta enjoy it jus fine!"

You idiot! That's because, to a starving man, a Ritz cracker tastes like filet mignon and caviar.

"No, no, no," Reese interjected, not letting the issue go. "You think I'm uppity?"

She began shoveling the food into her mouth. "This is what uppity looks like!" she exclaimed as she aggressively began chewing to make room for more in her mouth. Yet when she went to swallow, she immediately projected a look of disgust. Reese's taste buds had discovered the lack of seasoning in the gruel she had just devoured. Her eyes bulged out as though she wanted to regurgitate, but she was committed to proving a point. By the time Reese had cleaned her plate, I was rolling on the ground in laughter in my mind.

"Does THIS look like I'm uppity?" she said to him, showing Cletus a clean plate before letting it fall on the ground.

Talk about a drop-the-mic moment.

Cletus' eyes widened. "Woeman, is ya crazy?"

Reese closed the distance and bucked up to him.

"Call me...an uppity nigga. One. More. Time. And you're going to find out!"

Cletus wasn't a small guy, but he wasn't the biggest one, either. Knowing Reese was serious and determined, he considered his options and looked over to me for aid. I offered none.

If you can't run with the big dogs, then stay the hell on the porch!

Cletus began to back up. When he had receded a reasonable distance, he said, "Whun ya'll finish, I'll be waitin' outsad ta tac ya'll whur ya'll be workin'."

Nguyen and Porras looked over at each and became consumed with rancorous laughter. Shirley just stared at all of us as though we were insane.

"I'm sorry I lost it, Dr. Mazique," Reese said, attempting to quell her anger. "I just have a hard time being called a nigga, much less one who is uppity."

I warned her. "Watch what you say to Cletus. I believe him to be the slave master's bootlicker."

Porras, breaking his trademark silence, uncharacteristically spoke. "His what?"

"His minion and spy on the plantation."

"Oh."

Suddenly, an old, country female voice said, "Dat ain't da one ya gat ta fare. Whach out fo da cracka Mista Clark."

The statement had come from Shirley. She had appeared so detached no one had thought she was paying attention to our conversation.

"The what called Mr. Clark?" Nguyen asked, confused by both her country dialect and terminology.

I felt a need to translate.

"A cracker is a derogatory term for someone who is White. But there is some debate as to where it originated. It has existed since Shakespearean times and came from the Irish and the Scots. Back then, a cracker meant someone who was a braggart or a fast talker. Later in America, the term came to refer to poor southern Whites—in states like Kentucky, Georgia, and South Carolina—who were low-class farmers. Some of these same poor Whites were hired out to slave owners as overseers.

"These overseers, though on the bottom rung of the social ladder, considered themselves above free Blacks or slaves and often demonstrated their contempt in a brutal fashion. In the Black community, 'cracker' supposedly became a pejorative because the managers of the fields would crack their whips across any slave's back who was rebellious or not industrious enough with his or her work. I think Shirley is telling us to watch out for the White overseer whose name is Mr. Clark."

Shirley nodded in agreement.

A racist fun fact from your local anger translator: While the term "cracker" is a pejorative for someone who is White and racist, the term "soda cracker" is a derogatory word used to describe someone who is White and pretends to be liberal, but is secretly or subconsciously racist on the inside.

The term "saltine cracker" is a pejorative for a White person who is salty and mad. For better clarity on the latter, please refer to most of the people involved in the January sixth Capitol riot. I now return you to your featured program...

Getting one in on me, Porras quipped, "Thanks for that explanation. I knew you'd be good for something."

Reese turned to Shirley. "When you say to watch out for Mr. Clark, just how bad is he?"

The slave responded animatedly. "He bad juju! He bad juju!"

The word "*juju*" got my attention.

"Shirley," I intently questioned, "were you born a slave or were you born free in Africa?"

She lowered her head and paused for a second as though she were ashamed. She then defiantly said, "Africa is home. Da White demons steal me, whun I wus lattle, and brung me hur. Now I only spake dare spake 'cause I don't 'member my own."

I became giddy. "Are you from West Africa? What tribe? Can you remember?"

"I 'member. I am YORUBA and mi REAL name is Ngozi!" she proudly proclaimed. It felt like she hadn't been able to say that in quite a while.

I can only speak for myself, but upon hearing her declaration I became all warm and tingly on the inside.

Since we were having a touchy-feely moment, I figured I would take the time to find out if our group could trust Shirley—I mean, Ngozi. We had said a couple of things in front of her we probably shouldn't have.

"Ngozi, was Cletus born in Africa or was he born here, in slavery?"

"Cletus a nigga."

"I know he's a slave," I retorted, thinking Ngozi misunderstood me, "but was he born free or was he born in Africa?"

"Africa dun't mack menfolk like dat. Dis place do. Cletus a nigga! Not all slaves burn hur are niggas, but Cletus IS a nigga. Dun't truss 'em. He do whateva massa say do betta than massa eva could hisself."

Well, it looks like we can trust Ngozi.

When we turned to leave, she grabbed Reese's arm.

"Sorry I gav ya food dat tast like dat. I did nut knew who I wus makin' it fo an I dun't lack Cletus."

She went and grabbed a plate of food that had been set aside for someone else. Perhaps it was her own meal?

"Sat durn an have sum wild yams and hoecake wit me."

Reese eating hoecake? Imagine all of the jokes I could make about that!

It was a beautiful gesture. Ngozi was trying to make up for bad-tasting food. What she had made had probably been cooked out of spite, with everything being thrust upon her at the last minute. Add to this the fact she didn't like Cletus, who I'm sure was the one who delivered the message about feeding the plantation's slave guests. How could Reese turn her down? She looked at me for direction.

"It's fine, Reese," I told her. "Take about 15 minutes, eat and bond with Ngozi, then have her bring you to where we will be working. I'm sure Cletus won't mind your absence when we walk outside."

"Thank you, Dr. Mazique."

I grinned. "No. Thank YOU for not taking Cletus' head off, although if you had I wouldn't have been too regretful. Right now, he's not on my top 10 favorites' list. But since you WERE about to throw paws, I do have a question I've been meaning to ask since stepping through the portal."

"What is it?"

I hesitated for a second before asking, "Can you fight? I mean, it might be useful information if we ever get into a physical altercation with someone or some group."

Reese put her hand on her hip. "Are you asking because I'm a woman, or because you really want to know? Would you ask Nguyen or Porras if THEY could fight?"

She has a point. Use your rhetorical Jedi-powers to get you out of this #MeToo trap in which you've ensnared yourself.

"If they were as pretty as you?" I questioned before strategically pausing. "Yes, I would."

That's why you're the professor! Watch her back up like a bad tax return!

Reese blushed a little, even though she didn't want to. "You're good, you know that?" she replied patronizingly. "For the record, while I STILL think that question was sexist, I will give you a pass because of the excellent respond. You ARE right. I AM fine as hell!

"But to answer your question, can I fight? Let's just say this: Major Lewis and I are together for a reason. I might not be able to cause the mass destruction of which he is capable, but I'm FAR from ANYONE'S undercard. That's all you need to know. So now, Dr. Mazique, my counter-question to you is, can you keep up?"

I didn't answer. Instead, a wry grin overcame my face as I motioned to Nguyen and Porras that it was time to leave.

Can I keep up? You're damn skippy I can! And the real test might be to see which one of us can knock Cletus out first.

Chapter Fifteen
the cotton fields

From what I could tell, the plantation wasn't the biggest, but it wasn't exactly the smallest, either. It had approximately 35 slaves, six of which appeared too old to do much work. This included Shirley. Even slaves who were advanced in years were not spared from labor, though. Some brought water to those who worked in the fields. Others did the cooking or cleaning in the slave master's house.

From what I could tell, there was more than enough work for the other fully abled slaves. The plantation had hogs to slop, chickens to wrangle, and cows to milk. Of course, while I was not a master of any of these, I was familiar enough, having gotten previous experience in Arkansas when I was little, to hold my own. Perhaps, then, it was wishful thinking I would end up doing one of those three chores.

Be honest. You just wanted to play with udders.

Instead, I—along with Nguyen and Porras—was taken to the fields to pick cotton with the other field hands. Reese joined us a brief time later. She raved about the food Shirley had let her taste upon our departure. Despite that happy moment, the whole vibe of the day was weird...almost creepy.

Really? You are a professor and all you can say is the entire day felt weird and creepy? I would have said it seemed both surreal and anticlimactic. That's closer to the truth and it makes you appear more professional and intelligent. Come on, do I have to continue to carry this whole story?

For the entire day, McGovern was missing in action as we worked the fields. While his absence brought more questions than answers, we weren't able to contemplate long about him or his whereabouts. The movements of the overseer named Mr. Clark had us all on edge. A slim, wiry, older White man of medium height, he was terror and mayhem on two legs, appearing seemingly mad at everything. Or maybe he just had a bad attitude?

Tell me. How many overseers do you know who had a GOOD attitude? I think that's why the slave owners employed them.

The first thing I noticed about Clark was the way he strode around the slaves as if his shit didn't stink and he dared anyone to get out of line. The second thing, or rather things, I noticed about him were the elongated knife and bullwhip affixed to one side of his person, with a Colt model 1862 pistol revolver on the other. The vibe Clark gave off let others know he was more than willing to use any of them on a rebellious slave. I could see from the exposed body parts of some they had at least experienced his whip.

Yeah, whips tend to leave a long-lasting impression. Imagine that!

The third thing I noticed about Clark was the color of the gums in his mouth. They were stained black from dipping snuff.

For those not versed in southern culture, snuff can be both a hard and powdery form of finely ground tobacco, sometimes inhaled through the nostrils or put between the cheek and gums. Putting snuff in the mouth requires the users to frequently empty their unwanted juices into a spittoon.

Believe me, it is not the most hygienic or tantalizing thing to look at someone doing. Imagine a mouth full of tobacco juice and hawking it out every couple of minutes into a can. Now, keep that same picture in your mind and come and give me a kiss, baby!

Most of the time, Clark sat atop a horse, looking down on the workers, ready to gallop nowhere fast, to dish out the punishment for perceived injustice of backtalk or unsteady work. Cletus—ever the toady—brought our group over to the overseer early in the morning once Reese had joined us.

Before I get to that, though, I have to discuss the actions of Cletus. While I don't like to ever use the word, Shirley was right when she called Cletus...a...

If you're too ashamed to say it, then I will! Shirley was right when she called Cletus a nigga. He kissed Mr. Clark's ass all day and went around snitching on all of the other slaves, too! It's not like the overseer could be everywhere at once and see everything at once, but apparently, that's why Cletus was around, with his skinning and grinning ass. I wonder. Is this how Black folk started tap dancing for the man? Doesn't Cletus realize he will always be looked at as the dancing monkey? Sellouts are NEVER respected by their puppeteers. I should have gassed Reese up to bust him in the jaw when I had the chance.

When Cletus brought us up to Clark, he made sure to lower his head and dip slightly as though he were addressing a king.

"Massa Clark, dese da guess' slaves. Whatca wan me ta do wit dum?"

For some reason, the theme from *Jaws* began playing in my head. The birds in the distance, along with every other animal or insect, seemed to cease making any noise in the background. The overseer slowly, deliberately, stared us up and down with contempt, turning up his lip as though we had made his butt itch in discomfort.

"Put dem wit da otha niggas in da field," Clark finally said. "Teach dem how ta peck cotton."

Just like the men had done when coming from out of the county office building with McGovern, Clark began to glare at us oddly, as though we were more curiosities than slaves. Don't get me wrong. It's not as if he busted out into a wide grin; anyone could tell he was still as mean as a junkyard dog. Yet this dog was more than willing to sniff around before biting. I could tell we were playthings to

Clark, but how and why? Again, my thoughts ran back to McGovern. Had he said something about us being from the future? Surely, he wasn't that stupid.

Once again, we ARE talking about McGovern.

I was broken from my thoughts by Reese, who was crying out in pain from getting jabbed by the sharp edge of a boll.

"You know, Dr. Mazique," she told me softly as she held her hand, "I don't know if I'm going to make a good slave."

Before I could respond with a rhetorical pick-me-up, there was a sudden hiss through the air and then the sound of a sharp pop. Next came a distressing scream from one of the female slaves. Apparently, she hadn't been picking cotton fast enough. The oversized work dress she had on was ripped from where Clark's whip had just taken out a chunk of her flesh. Red blood marks splattered on the backside of her garment.

"Use niggas ned to wark a lil hardar!" roared Clark as he pulled back his whip. He looked over in our direction and began smiling at Reese. Had that demonstration in violence been for her?

"On second thought," she whispered, "I think I'll give this cotton picking another try."

Clark continued to glare at us but went around nitpicking the work ethic of the other slaves. No one was able to collect enough cotton fast enough to appease him, so a few more were viciously beaten. The tragic part is everyone seemed used to being stricken. The four of us were the only ones who were so shocked at what was going on that we actually stopped in astonishment to view the terror. To the other slaves, the whippings were business as usual, something to which they had grown accustomed.

It took a minute for me to catch on, but Clark was punishing the other slaves because of us, because of our collective lack of productivity. If this continued, after a while this would build up anger toward our group. Was that the real reason Clark was doing it or was there something else afoot? I tended to believe the latter, but the definitive answer still lay with McGovern. Surprisingly, I had improved in picking cotton. It seems my prior experience in Arkansas had proved invaluable. Now that I was older, I knew how to grab the bolls without getting stabbed and was faster harvesting them.

Nguyen, Porras, and Reese, however, sucked at picking cotton. There was simply no other way to say it. They were so slow the cotton could have grown at a faster rate than they collected it. The biggest obstacle to being quicker was not having on any gloves. Learning to pick cotton without a pair was not for the faint of heart.

The three of them struggled all day. Adding to their misery, the perfect posture for picking cotton is being bent over close to a 45-degree angle. This brings more stress and pain to bodies that aren't used to doing that kind of work. By noon, the three were all but exhausted, with still much of the day ahead. While I was not exactly full of energy, since I had had prior experience with picking cotton, I was not as tired because I knew how to pace myself. When lunch came, Nguyen, Porras, and Reese took a needed respite.

I saw Clark in the distance glaring at them, laughing at their energy-depleted bodies. Somehow, some way, he knew they were like fish out of water struggling to find their way. He was bound and determined to play psychological warfare, torturing them every step.

Some of the older slaves, which included Shirley, came to serve food to the field hands. We were given cornmeal and salted fish. I could tell Reese wanted to complain about the food selection—her arms were twitching—but she was too nervous, scared, and hungry to do so. Regardless, a ravenous piranha couldn't have cleaned its plate as fast as she did.

I guess Cantaloupe booty got over her aversion to slave food, huh? Being hungry as hell will do that to a person.

Cletus didn't seem to have to do the same work as the other slaves. As a matter of fact, he didn't do ANY physical work, except for walking around tattling on everyone. Doing no physical work is probably why he had the energy to tell on everyone. Later, I had every intention of correcting Shirley that Cletus wasn't a nigga; he was the plantation snitch.

Now you are telling it like it is!

Many plantations had slaves with such Stepin Fetchit mentalities. Such mindsets were something slave masters promulgated amongst their workforce to keep them in check. Playing slaves against one another cut down on the number of rebellions.

Indeed, one of the most draconian slave laws ever erected, the **Meritorious Manumission Act of 1710**, encouraged slaves to rat on one another. The law guaranteed a slave freedom under several conditions: 1) Saving the life of the slave master 2) Creating an invention from which the slave master profited 3) Telling on a slave or slaves who planned to revolt or run away. The last component of the decree is another major reason why none of the slave rebellions in the United States were ever successful.

A slave ratted out the others in every case. **Gabriel's Conspiracy**? Rat. **Denmark Vessey's Rebellion**? Rat. **Nat Turner's Rebellion**? Rat. John Brown's raid on **Harper's Ferry**? Rat. When people wonder why the Black community in the present can't seem to come together as a race, they have to understand the social conditioning done to them in the past. Of course, someone like McGovern would say I was using the **MMA** as an excuse. While part of his objection would be valid, I don't bring up things like the **MMA** for sympathy or excuses, only for understanding.

When lunch was over, Nguyen, Porras, and Reese had a look of horror on their faces. For some reason, they didn't think they would have to do more work so soon.

What part of being a slave did they not understand? Slaves don't get PTO or happy hour!

Gathering up their strength, the trio lethargically moved back into position. Had I not been a part of the group, I would have laughed at them myself. They were a pitiful work bunch, the military's finest beaten down in a couple of hours from the practice of picking cotton. Notwithstanding the others' defeat in the fields, inwardly I was proud of myself.

Though I would never be able to rival the output of work demonstrated by my uncles and aunts, I had finally found my inner family work ethic. I could now go back to my kinfolk in the present, work amongst them, and not embarrass myself. This private epiphany, however, did nothing to motivate my comrades. By the time the sun went down and the workday had ended, Nguyen, Porras, and Reese were like walking zombies, awkwardly plodding back and forth. After checking with Clark,

Cletus was instructed to return us to the slave cabins. He did as he was told, but I noticed during our walk back he made sure to stay far away from Reese. Cletus didn't have to be wary. Reese was so worn out she probably would have fallen asleep had she attempted to throw a punch.

During the trek to the slave cabins, I informed Nguyen and Porras the group needed to talk. Since we had been heavily observed during the day, neither Reese nor myself had been able to tell the two about Major Lewis' visit and Cletus' spying on us the night prior. I urged them to wait a while before knocking on our cabin door.

I wanted to make sure the snitch was nowhere around. It was then Reese told us Shirley had invited us back to her cabin for more food. Apparently, the two had hit it off and this newfound comradery had kept Shirley in her feelings about the bad breakfast. She wanted to atone with the whole group. Besides the fact we were all hungry, I thought meeting at Shirley's cabin and talking there was better.

Cletus tried his darndest to ear-hustle our conversation, but whenever I found him straying too close, I would guide everyone over toward Reese. She might have been as exhausted as a broke-legged dog, but she still gave him the stank eye, which was more than enough to keep Cletus away.

How are you going to be the plantation snitch AND be a coward? If you're going to go around telling on everyone, be prepared to defend yourself! The slave master can't protect you all of the time.

"So," Porras asked as he pulled a chicken leg from out of his mouth, "you REALLY think Major Lewis has all of this intel he says he has on McGovern?"

Thinking more about the chicken being served to us than the matter at hand, I replied, "I don't know."

I still hadn't touched my plate despite the aroma filling Shirley's shack. The food it was coming from looked and smelled absolutely scrumptious. My hesitation in eating wasn't because I thought the food was poisoned or something like that. I simply couldn't stop wondering from where Shirley had gotten the chicken. I had urged Reese to have Shirley wait outside while we talked and ate. That way, she would be able to stand watch for Cletus' backstabbing ass and have plausible deniability just in case things went awry. I would ask her about the chicken once we were done.

Tell the audience the really nerdy, geeky, history reason you were fixated more on the chicken than on figuring out the whole apocalyptic time disaster you SHOULD have been focused on preventing.

As I had told Reese, slaves didn't have access to an abundance of protein. While some were allowed to keep livestock like pigs and chickens—depending on the generosity of the slave master—I hadn't seen any near Shirley's cabin, nor anywhere near any of the other slave quarters, although I HAD seen what appeared to be several chicken coops closer to the plantation house where the slave master stayed.

Obviously, Shirley was one of the plantation cooks, a position probably given to her partly because of her advanced age. Yet I knew there was no way in hell the slave owner would have given her chickens to cook so the four guest slaves would have meat to eat.

Why not? Isn't chicken and watermelon all Black people eat, anyway? Maybe he was playing to stereotypes? Now you have me thinking about all of the money Popeye's Chicken could have made off Black people had they opened a franchise back in the day!

It was then I remembered something Frederick Douglass had mentioned in his narrative about when he was young and had been a slave. His mother had once awakened his brothers, sisters, and himself late at night to serve the family some chicken. He did not know from where she had gotten it but suspected she had stolen it from their slave master's farm. I now began to suspect the same thing of Shirley and I became scared for her.

Whatever McGovern had told the plantation master about us, he knew we were not normal slaves. Even if McGovern had not revealed everything, our movements about the plantation would still have been heavily scrutinized. As they were now, Cletus was attempting to keep an added eye on us, but was that the only snitch? Were there others? I didn't want Shirley getting mixed up, beaten and whipped, for befriending and helping us. I didn't want to put her life in danger.

Yeah, but that food sure did smell good, didn't it?

I finally started eating my food as much from starvation as from appreciation of Shirley's actions. It didn't take long before the chicken, okra, and black-eyed peas she had cooked found their way into my belly.

Don't feel guilty. If Shirley was bound to get beat later, you were obligated to eat the food. That way, she wouldn't get beat for nothing!

Reese, full as a tick and moving as slow as a three-toed sloth, lay on the ground with her back against a wall. She had long since inhaled her food. Now, the itis had developed in her.

"One thing I can say about Major Lewis," she said, "is that he doesn't lie. If he said he has intel against McGovern, he has intel against McGovern. At the very least, we know SOMETHING is up with the man. I mean, where has he been all day? Why did he suddenly start acting funny...more than he was acting before he went into the county courthouse?"

I added, "Did any of you notice how the White men started behaving once McGovern came from out of the building?"

"They didn't treat us like the rest of the slaves," Reese stated. "It was weird. It was like McGovern had told them we were from a foreign country and they were just sitting back observing how different we were from the rest of the Blacks."

It was time to face the elephant in the room; one, apparently, only I realized.

"No. It was like McGovern had told them the truth, that we were from their future on a quest to stop a crazed Black man from turning things even more on their head than they already are."

Everyone became dead silent.

"Are you sure?" Porras asked.

"Consider the facts," I retorted. "Do you think Clark would have had a problem beating any one of us? I mean, if we go by the plantation's standards of being productive early niggas, we got the early part right, but the productive part? Not so much. You all saw Clark whip a slave five times just for smiling, just for someone seeming to have one damn moment of solace! Who knows what was going through that slave's mind at the time he was smiling? Maybe he was thinking about a good night's sleep or a good meal. Whatever the case, Clark beat him just for taking a moment to smile. So, I ask you once more to consider the facts.

"He didn't touch us because he was in observation of us. He wanted to see how we would function, and wouldn't you if you were in his shoes? We are from his future, where we are free citizens and equal just like him. But here, in this period, we have to act like slaves, even though we aren't. Clark put us through a hamster wheel and laughed the entire time."

Reese thought about what I had just said. "That would explain why he looked at me the way he did."

"Exactly. He was playing with you and playing with us. I'm not saying Clark isn't a sonofabitch—you saw his actions—but half of those slaves today he beat because of us. He wanted to sow resentment to keep them from aligning with us."

"Why would any of the slaves align with us?" Nguyen asked.

"Because we are different. Because we represent hope. Don't forget, a war is now being fought over slavery, although in our present some will simply label it as the *War of Northern Aggression*. Slave owners are paranoid right now. Besides, our presence was enough to entice Shirley into stealing a chicken from the slave master to feed us this meal, and she just met us! Imagine what the others would do if we spent more time around them."

Porras looked down at his empty plate. "That chicken was stolen? Well, it sure was good, especially for a stolen piece of poultry!"

Reese asked, "How do you know it was stolen?"

"Do you see any chickens laying eggs outside of her cabin?" I flippantly responded. "You don't and that's because Shirley HAS no chickens!"

Again, there was silence.

Porras looked over at Nguyen. "Well, I think I can speak for both of us," he said. "You're right. Something IS up with McGovern. We all know he's shady. A dark cloud seems to follow him. The way he talks and acts, he's probably racist too. And while both of those things don't necessarily make him guilty, it's enough to make me hit pause, grab him, and see what Major Lewis has."

"So, what's the plan?" Reese questioned.

I contemplated for a second before saying, "McGovern HAS to appear at some point. I say we wait, albeit impatiently. When we see him, we somehow coerce him to come with us, while creating distance between us and this plantation."

Nguyen raised a good point. "What about our weapons?"

"Normally, I would be afraid about leaving anything from the future behind," I explained, "but under the circumstances? We can't just walk up to the slave master and demand our things back. The future might already be screwed, anyway, with all of our interactions we've had with people from the past. It's just best if we nab both Lewis and

McGovern and get back to the present to see what has already been affected and how to best fix it."

"What happens if we get into a situation where it looks like we might have to fight?"

"Then we fight. It's that simple. But now that you've brought the subject up, just what can you two do? I've been told you're both bad asses."

Nguyen started smiling. "I do alright for myself."

I pointed to Porras. "And your buddy here?"

"He's a freaking Aztec warrior!"

Porras's face contorted as he began to reprimand his colleague. "How many times must I remind you? I'm MEXICAN AMERICAN! I'm not AZTEC!"

"So? You used to call me Genghis Khan when we first met!"

"Well, what was wrong with that?"

"Genghis Khan was Mongolian! I'm Chinese!"

"At least both of you are Asian! Can you at least gas me up based on someone with ties to Mexico?"

"Well, I guess I can call you Poncho Villa."

"So why don't you?"

Nguyen fell out laughing. "Because it won't piss you off like it pisses you off when I call you a freaking Aztec warrior!"

Unfortunately, the occasion of levity was cut brutally short. There was a sudden scream from the outside which instantly sucked away the silliness and deliberation of the moment, giving everyone a chill deep within their souls. The sound was not so much a shriek of pain and anguish as it was of horror and despair. I wasn't sure, but it sounded as if it had come from Shirley.

WTF?

Without thinking, we all clumsily jumped to our feet and piled towards the door. Once outside, we immediately regretted being there. Greeted with a barrage of burning torches and kerosene lamps, our eyes took a few seconds to adjust, but when they did, we gasped for air. The reality of our situation seem like a stiff, strong punch had collided with our stomachs.

Off to one side, Shirley lay hopelessly on the ground, with Clark standing over her with his bullwhip; off to the other, Cletus stood by himself holding onto a torch, attempting to look tough. But the thing really giving us chills was what stood directly in front of us: Approximately a dozen White men, with pistols and guns in their hands, who all had crudely-made Klan hoods over their faces. McGovern, still wearing the same clothes from earlier, and without a hood, was among them.

If I had been prone to pee my pants at any point in my life, right then would have been the opportune time to become R. Kelly.

He condescendingly spoke, "Good evening, Dr. Mazique. First, the slave master has the matter of a stolen chicken to resolve. Then, once that's taken care of, all of us are going for a long walk where we will talk about the future of this country."

Oh, hell no! Now, the shit has REALLY hit the fan!

Chapter Sixteen
when the shit hit the fan

In the name of equity—and because I think I am a better storyteller—I will be commandeering much of this chapter. I hope this action isn't too disconcerting. If it is, I'm sorry you feel that way.

I see you are maturing. Before this little adventure, you would have told me to kiss your ass.

Now look at who is doing all of the cursing!

I'm NOT cursing. I simply said what the OLD you would have said.

I resent that and I'm offended. The OLD me would not have said that. You need to apologize.

Apologize? You DO realize you are a part of my subconscious and it would be asinine to apologize to myself?

That's YOUR problem, not mine. Is this how you treat someone who was with you when McGovern and his henchmen showed up to get biblical on you and the others?

Um...you kinda HAD to be with me during all of that; again, you are my subconscious! Why am I even arguing with you, anyway? Are you going to narrate this chapter or what?

Yes, but...let me ask you something first.

Sigh. What is it?

How REAL can I be?

Now you have ME saying, WTF?

I only ask that question because I want the readers to actually feel what you experienced and, don't take this personally, sometimes you fall short in that department. It's like you have this intimate moment, with a lot of build-up, but a poor finish. Now I see why women get mad with men who sell wolf tickets. You let your professionalism get in the way of the delivery. Let your emotions fly!

Maybe that's because I want the readers to understand the story and not get caught up with a bunch of cuss words and an incoherent mass of verbal masturbation.

I'm wounded you think so low of me. I am a part of you; therefore, I must be a part of the sum. Just...trust me on this. I think you will be surprised by my presentation.

I will be surprised when you stop with all of this bovine defecation.

So that means I can't be real in telling the story?

Since you are REALLY getting on my nerves right now, and since this is going on like a broken record, you just do you. Okay? Be as real as death and taxes. Just. Tell. The. Damn. Story.

Kewl.

✳✳✳

I won't lie. I thought we were ALL going to die! And that was going to be a shame, too. I would have hated to meet my demise without serving several people a knuckle sandwich. Cletus was first on that list, although I wouldn't have been too mad if Reese had beaten me to the proverbial punch. It would serve him right to get manhandled by a woman.

Yeah, I know, that sounds sexist—and it IS—but so what? The reality is, no man wants to get beat down by a woman, especially by a pretty one. A man will only accept getting beat down by a woman if her name is Brunhilda, she raises oxen in the Himalayas, and has an egregious amount of hair growing from out of her nose and armpits.

McGovern was at the top of the knuckle sandwich list. My conscious side had tried to give him the benefit of the doubt, but by showing up like this with these men in hoods, he had confirmed everything Major Lewis had said about him. What were they supposed to be, anyway, the Cro-Magnon KKK? Technically, the real Klan wouldn't debut for another three years.

The men and McGovern took Shirley and us further away from the plantation, really deep into the woods. They didn't want the rest of the slaves to bear witness to what was going to occur. Although the torches and illumination of the kerosene lamps in the night caused a few heads to peek from out of their cabin doors, Cletus the Snitch quickly ushered them back inside with threats of retaliation by Clark and the slave master.

My heart beat feverishly and fear made my adrenaline flow like cow piss on a flat rock. I now faced the fear of every Black man: Being marched in the darkness of the night by hooded racists who not only despised my existence, but the very air I breathed. I hated I was powerless against my oppressors, just like my ancestors had been powerless against their oppressors. Would these White men castrate me and hang me like the cowards they were? The unknown certainty of my future, the fear of my impending death, was debilitating.

Fear is a reaction while courage is a choice.

So, I chose not to give in to my fear. I embraced the moment and stared every one of those SOBs in their faces with an expression that said, "Bring it on, baby, bring it on."

I wanted to talk some fly, '60s, gritty Dolomite shit to my captors, but talking shit when you don't have the upper hand will get you pumped full of shit, and then you're dead as shit. So, I just chilled. I looked at Reese and, while she was poised, both of her arms were twitching like a crackhead who had just taken a hit of some really good stuff. Nguyen and Porras had the look of military determination. However, their expression also included a smattering of disappointment.

They, too, had wanted to give McGovern the benefit of the doubt. He was, after all, their superior officer. But how did he get so high in rank and be such a racist? Didn't he swear an oath to protect and serve this nation, which includes its people and its laws?

Now YOU'RE the one acting brand new! What does all you say mean? Weren't the people who brought Africans on a vacation cruise against their wills to the Americas supposedly Christian, too? Our nation's history is rife with hypocrites. Don't act as if McGovern is Christopher Columbus. He's just another Johnny-come-lately bigot who says one thing but does another.

I couldn't tell who the plantation's slave owner was because most of the men had on hoods. Clark took the lead on dealing with Shirley and it was not a sight I wanted to see. Smiling devilishly, he all but barbarically skull-drug the slave—who was kicking and screaming like a wild animal—across the ground towards a tree.

What he was intending on doing to her, she wasn't going to make easy. When Clark hustled Shirley and forced her to stand up, she took the opportunity to smash him across the mouth with a hard-thrown right hand. I have to give Clark credit, though. Shirley was a big, The Color Purple-looking woman.

The punch colliding with his face would have downed a normal man. Clark, though, was too damn mean and racist to be taken out by someone Black, much less by a Black woman. Staggering, it took him a split second to recover. Once he did, he blasted Shirley with a couple of punches of his own. She finally went down to the ground like a bad habit.

As she did, Clark picked up a nearby stick of some girth and beat her in the head with it until it broke. And this was all because of some chicken she had stolen to cook for us. Popeyes be damned! Clark then forced her to stand back up—blood dripping profusely from her head—before slamming her against a nearby oak tree of tremendous size. He made her hug it, wrapping each of her arms halfway around, before using rope to circle the rest to secure her arms. All Nguyen, Porras, Reese, and I could do is look on in dismay and hopelessness.

I don't think I can quite convey how hard it was looking at Shirley being brutalized. The whippings of several of the female field hands earlier were nothing compared to this. Clark would never beat a field hand this savagely because anyone beaten like that could not work. Since she was old, anyway, her slave master probably didn't care whether she lived or died. He had to set a macabre example. Stealing chickens was an affront he would not tolerate.

As someone who knew the history of Black women in America, I was beyond being sick and tired of even HEARING of a Black female being persecuted, much less WATCHING it in real-time. The sight made me ill to my stomach and want to cry, not because of sadness but because of anger. At that moment, I had no way to release or display my frustrations. And with an absence of weapons, there was no way we could protect Shirley.

This feeling built up a special kind of motivation for revenge in me. I never wanted to be that man, that Black man who couldn't defend a woman from a sometimes cruel and savage world. The only thing from which I could never detach myself when teaching history was the nation's treatment of Black women. Everything else—the stories of the Middle Passage and the lynching of Black men—never consumed me.

Because of my knowledge of history, though, I know the full story of how Black men could never protect their women during slavery, even if they were married. I had read the slave narratives and seen enough differing hues of my people—light, bright, and damned near white—to know the slave masters had raped and beaten Black women with impunity, thinking it was their birthright. I had often wondered how Black women viewed Black men during that era and, conversely, how black men viewed themselves.

If Black men couldn't protect their women, did

they truly view themselves as men? And how did Black women view them? As men or as boys?

It takes a special kind of man to beat an innocent woman: The kind who is evil and is destined for Hell. Likewise, it takes a different breed of men who would stand around laughing at that sort of thing. But that's all the hooded and unhooded mob was doing. McGovern, who was standing approximately 20 feet away from our group, sadistically observed our reactions with much satisfaction.

Five men stood directly behind us with pistols and rifles pointed at our backs. McGovern had told them to shoot anyone who closed their eyes, lowered their head, or looked away from Shirley getting whipped. The rest of the mob stood on the other side of the tree. They moved in close to see Shirley getting tortured as if a difference of a couple of feet would make their viewing pleasure more memorable.

She screamed and cursed them all as she was getting beaten, both in English and, I guess, in Yoruba as well; I couldn't make out the dialect, she was in so much pain. Shirley was strong, though, both physically and spiritually. It took 15 lashes—15 hard, penetrating lashes—before she went silent, and it took five more before she stopped moving. I didn't think she was yet dead, only unconscious. With her hands tied around the tree, she was prevented from falling onto the ground.

Her body just sort of slumped against the big oak,

all evidence of her earlier cacophonic anguish gone. But honestly, the only reason I think Clark stopped whipping her was because his arm had gotten tired. The brief struggle with her minutes earlier had taken a lot out of him.

Clark was no spring chicken and Shirley had hit him with all of the strength of a full-grown man. Seeing victory within his grasp, McGovern took the opportunity to strut forward and fully reveal himself. He was a general and he had an audience.

"How are you doing this evening, Dr. Mazique?" he smugly asked, coming up to me with a boastful expression. I noticed all of the White men tuning in to see how I would reply. They wondered, just what does a Black man from the 21st century sound like?

Still in my Superfly mind state, my initial reaction was to tell McGovern his momma said I was doing great, but I didn't think the time had come for me to go there.

"You know me, General," I retorted. "As well as I can be seeing an innocent woman getting beaten."

McGovern's eyebrow went up. "Innocent, you say?" he pointed to a hooded man in the middle of the mob. "Her slave master doesn't see it that way. He says she stole one of his chickens to feed you. Is that true?"

You know it's true, asshole.

"Yes."

"Well, I say that makes all of you about as guilty

as her."

Reese let out a growl, or at least it sounded like a growl. She was too pissed off to react any other way but viscerally. If I felt a certain kind of way about what I had just witnessed, she DEFINITELY felt a certain way.

"Back in our era, there are 34 million underfed Americans. Are you going to beat them if they steal a chicken to eat, too?"

His response was immediate and direct. "Only if they steal chickens to feed niggars or niggars steal them to feed themselves."

All the White men began to laugh.

I asked, "How does it feel to finally be able to use that word freely?"

Good question! I, too, have always wanted to know how a White person feels after using the N-word. I mean, do they experience feelings of euphoria, elation, or regret?

"You mean, how does it feel to not have to worry about being written up, reprimanded, dismissed from my position, or otherwise harassed and threatened on social media? Absolutely wonderful! I've ALWAYS said the word, just not out loud."

Strategic pause. "So, you ARE a Grand Wizard?"

McGovern vacillated as if in deep reflection. "I wondered if Major Lewis had been in contact with any of you. Now I know he has."

I looked over at Cletus before replying, "Don't act

like I slipped up and you just discovered something. You're not that brilliant. The slave master's minion already told you Major Lewis contacted us last night."

"Yes, he did, but he was unable to tell us just what the three of you discussed."

"Not much. Lewis just filled in the blanks about what I had been feeling ever since embarking on this mission."

Bursting into a guffaw, McGovern turned to the White men and said, "I told you this niggar was smart! You have to watch this one."

He turned back towards me. "And just what did you suspect?"

That when you go to the bathroom, you use a lot of toilet paper because you're full of shit!

"To coin a phrase some of my students use, that you were being a little extra."

"I was being a little extra?"

Yes: You were being extra hypocritical, extra racist, and an extra dumbass.

"You were being extra AND thirsty. First, it was weird for someone of your rank to be going on a mission like this. It was too dangerous a risk. So why were you really on it and who authorized you to go? Second, it was odd you would include Major Lewis' fiancée. Tactically and ethically, it didn't make sense.

"At the very least, it was a definite conflict of interest someone of your stature should have been aware. You didn't know where her loyalties lay. Love is a powerful thing. Historically, it has driven nations to war. How could you hazard that Reese would not betray you or the mission? I figured, more than likely you included her as bait, to lure Lewis out into the open. But the fact you would resort to such subterfuge told me something about your character.

"You were a sneaky, underhanded bastard. These two things alone put me on high alert. I knew I couldn't trust you because you had your agenda. And this was before we even stepped through the portal. Since I was already doubtful, I paid attention to everything else. The rest was easy to figure out. I just needed Lewis to verify what my naivety had prevented me from believing."

McGovern appeared impressed. I guess he had assumed the only thing Black men were capable of was drinking malt liquor and listening to rap music. Well, THIS Black man listened to Burt Bacharach, Bobby Blue Bland, and John Coltrane too!

"Please tell me," he questioned, much to my chagrin, "why was it so hard for you to believe?"

Should I turn into Dolomite now?

I sighed heavily before rebuking him. "Because I couldn't believe a general of the United States would betray his country."

Some of the White men who had been conversing amongst themselves became quiet. The talk of betraying the country struck close to home. It was the current resounding sticking point. What was the Civil War, if not an act of betrayal?

One culture turning on another to maintain a different way of life? The South didn't see it that way. They saw April 12, 1861, when the Confederate troops opened fire on Fort Sumter, as simply drawing a line in the sand over an issue that would have eventually led to war, anyway. Did the South not have a right to maintain their culture, no matter how brutally that right might manifest? No race has a right to subjugate and commit genocide against another to maintain a certain way of life.

McGovern almost choked on his laughter. "Betray the United States? I'm not trying to BETRAY the United States. I'm trying to SAVE it! Do you know what America has become? A refuge for the refuse of the planet.

"We've got immigrants marching North unchecked into the United States from all of these two-bit backwater, dictatorial South American countries. And we continue to let them in because the damn Democrats want to make everything look like the state of California. Meanwhile, Mexico can't seem to keep its pharmaceutical problem or cartels in check, so drugs and violence from that country continue to spill over into ours.

"Next, we're allowing too many Sand niggars in from too many Arabic countries: The same Arabs who want to blow us the hell off the map; the same Arabs who endorsed the terrorists who hijacked the planes which led to 9/11. But we can't turn them away because of all of the bleeding-heart liberals in Congress.

"Meanwhile, the military's ranks have become swelled with more niggars, gooks, japs, chinks, and Sand niggars. And if that wasn't enough, to make matters worse, now we have all of this LGBTQ+ crap to worry about! Did you know the military now has a lieutenant colonel who is transexual? That's embarrassing! In my opinion, a man who has his dick removed and now goes by 'she' and 'he' pronouns has no right to be in my military."

I looked at him pitifully and replied, "Despite that hullabaloo, I still don't understand how a penis, vagina, or him/her pronouns affects a person's ability to aim and fire a gun. All you've just described is a man who is paranoid about the changing landscape around him. You are a dinosaur from a begotten era that no longer exists. You long to maintain a period that simply refuses to die."

McGovern started grinning like the cat that had eaten the canary. He reached behind him into a bag to which I hadn't been paying attention and pulled out something bulky. Throwing it at my feet, the object landed with a loud thud.

Even though there was a lot of light from the torches and kerosene lamps, I couldn't tell what it was. Kicking at it, I discovered it was a book. Curious, I reached down to pick it up. When I saw the actual cover, I thought McGovern had lost his mind, not that he had much to work with from the start.

The book was Carol Reardon and Tom Vossler's 2016, **A Field Guide to Antietam: Experiencing the Battlefield Through its History, Places, and People**. *It was one of the best books available to help lay people in understanding some of the most brutal major battles of the Civil War. It discussed strategies, terrain, and resources used by generals on both sides. McGovern was planning the White version of* **Return to Nubia**.

I all but yelled, "Are you crazy? You brought a history book back in time? What in the hell were you thinking?"

"Since I don't have all of your knowledge of the past, Dr. Mazique," McGovern nonchalantly answered, "I thought I would level the playing field. I'm going to make sure the South won the war. As an added plus, to GUARANTEE it wins, I'm going to make sure the person who was the South's single biggest obstacle never exists."

WTF? I just knew he couldn't be referring to...

"I'm going to go back in time to erase General Ulysses S. Grant from existence."

I know what my conscious side said about time retaliating in some form or fashion if it were ever tampered with, but if Grant were taken off the board entirely, I had very little faith the North would ultimately triumph over the South. In my opinion, he was the sole reason Union forces had originally won. Before taking command, the North had been getting its proverbial ass kicked and the war was dragging out. Many economists believe the North would have eventually won because of access to more resources and more people, yet they miss the entire point.

Military strategists in the South KNEW they probably couldn't beat the North. They didn't need to. All they had to do was drag the war out—raise the body count—and the North would eventually capitulate and offer a truce. It would eventually have to cave into the demands of the South.

Enter the sloppy, unkempt, inebriated and seemingly inept General Grant. He never kept his uniform spiffy. Most of the time when he reported to work, it was rumpled and looked as if he had slept in it. Grant also liked liquor, although many historians state his need to tipple was exaggerated. Regardless, his battle acumen did not go unnoticed by President Lincoln. Where other Union generals had lacked the balls to go directly toe-to-toe with the South and were losing battles, Grant was running through the Confederate army like a hot knife through butter.

When Lincoln handed Grant the command of the

Union forces in 1864, Grant had a lot of haters telling Lincoln he was a drunk who didn't deserve the position and would fail. Though Lincoln should have told Grant's detractors which side of his white cheeks to kiss, he instead allegedly told them to find out what type of liquor Grant drank so he could give it to the rest of the North's generals. His logic was, if liquor had made Grant so great on the battlefield, then perhaps his other generals needed to tipple a little bit, too.

After this, Grant and General William Tecumseh Sherman synchronized and went to work like the Wonder Twins, taking apart the Confederate army. The rest is history. Well, it WAS history, but this racist bastard seeks to change all of that. Without Grant, the North was/is doomed.

There began to be restlessness among the mob. Too much talk was being exchanged and it needed its pound of flesh. A shudder went through me. I knew who would be the first to go.

"Dat niggar taks too match," one of the hooded men exclaimed.

"Yeah," another joined in, "and he's a tad bit uppity, too. Nothin' riles me up as match as an uppity niggar!"

A third screamed, "I say we hang his niggar black arse!"

It was at that moment I felt I had nothing to lose. I was proud my conscious side decided to let me off of my leash; a dog needs to be able to run around some time. I gave the White man who had just called for me to be hung my best Dolomite.

"No," I commanded, pointing at him, "why don't we hang YOUR White ass, instead?"

Everyone stopped gassing each other up and just stared at me, stunned. Perhaps they had never heard a Black man telling them to kiss his ass? Well, they had previously been dealing with slaves. I wasn't scared of them—maybe I was afraid to die—but I wasn't scared of them. I was a free Black man from their future. I held a doctorate, taught both Black AND White students, and watched Obama when he was in the White House. I KNEW what the future held, what the promise of America still holds.

*Since I knew I didn't have much time to speak before the mob came to its senses, I remembered a monologue given by a slave in the movie **Mandingo**, right before he was hung, and attempted to go with that same ride-or-die spirit.*

"Who are you inbred, racist, country fucks to stand in judgment of anyone? Especially since the majority of the backbreaking work in this country was done by people of color. Are you serious? Really? Then, just let me say this: When you hang me, you better make sure you hang me nice and tight.

"Make sure I'm as dead as your momma's decrepit, dirty drawers! Because, if you don't, I'm gonna go back in time and tell the Native Americans to kill up every damn Pilgrim who stepped foot on Plymouth Rock! And then I'm gonna back in time to Europe and remove Christopher Columbus' shriveled, two-inch, gonorrhea-laden penis and insert it up his ass and into his mouth!"

Astonishingly, the mob didn't respond too well to my Dolomite-like soliloquy. Who would have thought that? Perhaps they didn't like my delivery or they perceived my speech as a little too inflammatory?

"Shat dat niggar up!" a hooded man exclaimed. "Hang his black arse!"

A pair of hands quickly grabbed me from behind by the neck and I was aggressively pushed forward, towards the tree. Then, something odd happened. The force on my neck which was trying to manhandle me was suddenly gone. But without it to balance my body, the inertia from its initial push led me to stumble to the ground. Thinking whoever had grabbed me had simply lost his grip, I immediately sprung to my feet, ready to go down fighting as Shirley had. Yet when I looked back at my assailant, I saw a hooded man slowly staggering toward me, his white mask stained red from the splatter of blood, an arrow firmly halfway through his throat.

A second later, he plopped on the ground unmoving, dead. It was then that the shit hit the fan.

Hooded and unhooded alike peered into the night like terrified children. They had come prepared to be the terrorists, not the ones who would end up being terrorized. A hush fell over them, with most of the mob crouching down attempting to ascertain from where the danger might come.

Major Lewis had finally arrived.

I looked at Reese, who looked back at me and she began smiling. The five men still had their weapons trained on us, but it's really hard to stand guard over someone when you are peeping over your own shoulder, wondering whether or not an arrow will end up in your neck. Glancing at Nguyen and Porras, their eyes told me they were simply biding their time, hoping Lewis would allow them to strike.

Another arrow whizzed from out of the void of the night into another man's chest. As he fell backward, he let off a round from his rifle into the air. This errant blast was followed by a volley of gunshots from the remaining mob into the darkness of the forest. Everyone's head was on a swivel, looking around at nothing in particular, their paranoia making them antsy and their feet shuffle. Slowly, their numbers were being reduced. There were still nine men remaining, not counting McGovern and Cletus. The general then got an idea.

McGovern pointed at Reese. "Someone, grab that Black bitch! He won't do anything if we put a knife to her throat."

Even I knew that was a stupid move. You NEVER touch another man's woman: Especially when you don't know where in the darkness he's lurking. With one hand on his pistol and another reaching out towards Reese, a foolish man close to her tried to comply with McGovern's orders. Right before he made contact, an arrow was fired into one of his wrists.

"Aaah!" the man cried, dropping his gun onto the ground and immediately clutching the area around the wound. He didn't writhe in agony long. Another arrow found its way into his heart, putting him down for the count.

Out of our group, I thought it would be one of the men who would strike first. I was wrong. Clark wasn't too far from Reese when the first arrow found its mark. As the bloodletting continued, he had moved unwarily closer to her out of fear. After the last hooded man became a human porcupine, the men behind Nguyen, Porras, and Reese began to be too concerned for their well-being to keep their weapons focused on them. Reese saw her chance. She moved swiftly and stealthily, diving and rolling on the ground next to Clark with perfect timing.

She was such a badass! Rising to her feet, Reese snatched Clark's knife from his hip and stabbed him several times in quick succession in vital body areas. Clark never saw what was coming and didn't have a chance to react. Not waiting for him to fall, Reese left the knife in him and grabbed his pistol. She then instinctively put Clark's body in front of hers as a shield. Watching Reese move like poetry in motion as a killer finally made me overstand her connection to Lewis.

They were two sides of the same coin—male and female—physically, mentally, and spiritually bound: The yin to his yang. To have such a relationship is rare. But there is no way Lewis would have put the woman he loved in jeopardy unless he fully believed in his mission. Such passion in his stance made me reconsider. Was I wrong in attempting to stop him from changing the past? Especially since it was supposed to be in my people's favor?

The five men who had been standing guard, though slow to react, now trained their guns on Reese. Shots rang out in her direction, with a couple striking Clark's body. Reese made herself as small a target as she could, propping up the corpse and returning fire. One of her bullets pierced an unlucky man's hood. A red stain immediately spread from the hole it made.

When he fell, Nguyen and Porras became human action figures. They rushed the remaining four men and engaged them. Despite having no weapons, the two moved in close, making it difficult for their enemies to let off a shot without hitting one of their own. After a few seconds, Nguyen and Porras had disarmed them and were getting the upper hand.

Nguyen had been right. Porras was a freaking Aztec warrior! Moving so fast and with such precision, his opponents were blindsided. Unfortunately, his triumph would be short-lived. The remaining men on the other side by the tree, now less paranoid, had come to their senses. With visible targets to attack, they trained their remaining firepower on the three, while still watching out for errant arrows.

When Porras went to retrieve a discarded rifle from the ground, he was struck in his stomach by a bullet. Doubling over and smiling before falling, he looked at his comrade.

"Porras!" Nguyen yelled as he snapped the neck of a man with whom he had been struggling.

Reese fired at the hood who had just killed Porras, but missed. My eyes darted over towards McGovern, then towards Cletus. Neither had a gun in their hands. McGovern was too shell shocked his plans were going to shit to react. And Cletus the Snitch was Black. He didn't have a weapon because the White men weren't trusting enough to give him one. Since no bullets were flying by me and no one was currently paying any attention, I decided it was time I took my pound of flesh. I started with Cletus. It had been a long time since I had struck a man. The ramifications of my last street fight ended up with me facing serious jail time. I had almost killed someone.

My age, being 17 years old, wasn't going to save me. The court saw my prior Golden Gloves experience as someone whose hands were deadly weapons. It was only through the grace of God—and because of a lot of money that my mother had invested in retaining a good lawyer—that I was given a second chance. Before she died, I had promised her I would never strike another man. I vowed to turn my life around and dedicate it to school. Up until now, I had kept that promise.

However, if I were ever going to break a promise to my mother, it was going be for a damn good reason! This was a good reason. Even my mother would have agreed it was time to open up the old can of whoop-ass. She hated bullies and racists. McGovern was going to be my entrée, but right now I wanted an appetizer. Cletus was about 15 yards from me and his head was turned. It wouldn't have mattered if he had been looking my way; this just made the occasion sweeter.

I broke out into a sprint and, with perfect timing, caught him just as he turned his head when he heard my footsteps. I was almost drooling at the unobstructed target his jaw presented. Rarely had I been able to hit a man so cleanly and with so much force. Connecting to his jaw, my technique was sound; a textbook overhand right to the face. The blow interrupted Cletus' sinus, altering the flow of blood to his head. It also sent one of his teeth flying out of his mouth. The whole scene played out as if he had suddenly gotten struck with a sledgehammer. His head seemed to go one way as his body went another.

"That was for Shirley, you backstabbing bastard," I said, standing over him as he lay unconscious.

A bullet too close to my ear made my Black ass duck for cover. I scanned the area for McGovern. He was just now pulling out a weapon, a semi-automatic pistol he had brought back through the portal. A poor shot, he began gunning for Reese but probably couldn't hit the side of a barn if he were standing two feet away from it. Jesus! When was the last time McGovern had fired a weapon? I knew soccer moms who did a better job at handling one. And THIS is the man who wanted to create a White **Return to Nubia**? *He was going to lead it? I saw then McGovern couldn't lead anyone unless it was off a cliff. If the two ever meet, Nathan Bedford Forrest should smack McGovern upside his head for letting people know the two were affiliated.*

Meanwhile, on the other side of the conflict, Nguyen wasn't taking Porras' death well. The two had been paired for a long while, serving together through many military missions and conflicts. They had been through some pretty hairy ordeals. For his friend to get taken out under such bullshit circumstances was something he could not accept. Dying back in time, fighting a bunch of racists over history that already happened? Nguyen snapped. Call it regressed PTSD or whatever, but he snapped and went bonkers.

At that moment, I don't think he cared if he lived or died. He just wanted revenge and to take as many of them as he could. I can respect that. Porras would have been proud his old friend went out like a G. Frantically scanning the area for a weapon and finding none, Nguyen instead picked up a large stick and began making his way toward the rest of the forces.

Everyone was firing at Reese, who by now was running out of body; Clark's corpse was so riddled with bullets, his limbs had begun falling off. To protect herself, she had crouched down even lower, with the corpse barely being propped up against her. Having exhausted her ammunition, she couldn't defend herself. To make matters worse, it had been a few minutes since any arrows had flown through the air. The remaining men had become less apprehensive about becoming targets and were shooting at her unchecked.

Running toward the last standing hoods, Nguyen suddenly screamed, "I am the punishment of God! If you had not committed great sins, God would not have sent a punishment like me upon you!"

The rifleman hit Nguyen with a shot. His body jerked backward, but he kept running. Determination and adrenaline can sometimes make ordinary men supermen. A second rifle shot jolted him again, but by now it was clear Nguyen would at least make it to the men. If someone doesn't care whether they live or die, there is very little that can be done to deter them from their last acts.

The men with the pistols realized this as the distance between Nguyen and his intended targets closed. They became sloppy and nervous, shooting at him but missing by a mile. The rifleman couldn't get off another shot before Nguyen fell upon him. A wild swing with the stick of wood connected upon his first effort, the white sheet on the man's head immediately becoming red on one side as he collided with the ground. A bullet from a pistol entered Nguyen from behind.

Staggering, he turned and smote another man before stumbling. He swung at another, but the blood and energy were drained from his body. He felt his soul slipping and Porras on the other side. He finally collapsed from his injuries. Though I was sad about his death, I smiled inwardly. Nguyen's last act, what he yelled before he charged the men, had been a quote by Genghis Khan, once the most feared man on the planet. During his lifetime, he amassed the largest contiguous empire in the world.

When he went to war with a nation, his enemies

were given two choices: Surrender and become a part of the Mongol empire or die. Now, when Genghis Khan said to die, he wasn't just talking about you. He was talking about you, your mother, your father, your children, your dogs, AND your cats. You get the picture. Total annihilation. Talk about scary? Genghis was the epitome of the word. Now, can you picture someone with that type of reputation saying the same thing Nguyen yelled before charging the men?

Porras probably didn't know Nguyen knew anything about Genghis Khan, yet Nguyen had embraced the nickname, at least before his death. There was a certain poetry in that. To me, this is what America was about, a place where someone of Chinese descent and someone of Mexican descent could become friends, despite all of the political cacophony and social bullshit in the background.

This led me to conclude I was going to stick with my decision no matter what. The irony of the situation was that McGovern was the last person with any ammunition in his gun. The clicks of the pistols from the remaining two men alerted me to the fact they were empty. Once McGovern realized he was still in the driver's seat, he became emboldened and arrogant. There had been no sign of Lewis for a while, no arrows flying through the air. Perhaps he had run out of them? It didn't matter.

McGovern had a sly grin on his face and he pointed his pistol at Reese and then at me. Reese had long since abandoned her crouching stance, throwing Clark's body aside and was standing up. While we weren't next to each, we weren't far away from one another, either. Even with his non-shooting ass, McGovern would eventually strike one of us. I estimated he had about nine bullets or so left out of a 17-bullet clip.

Pointing his weapon at us, he huffed, "That's why I don't like niggars. Your kind always fucks shit up! Goddamn roaches, you people are worse than gremlins!"

I couldn't help myself. It was priceless seeing McGovern pissed off to the height of pisstivity itself.

"If you think THAT'S something," I quipped, "you should see what happens when you throw water on us!"

I became his target. He pointed his pistol at me.

"You!" McGovern screamed. "I'm tired of your smart niggar mouth, you Black sonofabitch!"

Despite impending death, for some reason, I still couldn't control my tongue. Maybe it's because I refused to let a bigot have the last word, even though he had a gun pointed in my direction and was hellbent on killing me.

"Which one am I? A smart-mouthed nigga or a Black sonofabitch? I MUST be a Black sonofabitch, because being a smart-mouthed nigga is an oxymoron. According to White people, niggas can't be smart, but they CAN be Black sonofabitches. Right?"

"Shoat his black arse!" one of the two remaining men shouted. "Shoat 'em!"

I saw my entire life flash before me. While I hadn't exactly thought it would end the way it appeared it was going to end, I wasn't regretful. Some people die in their sleep, others while they're eating. At least I was going to die doing something I loved: Being a part of history, not getting old and gathering dust in a rocking chair.

Then something miraculous happened: An arrow blazed from out of the darkness into McGovern's right hand. The two remaining men jumped backward in apprehension as the general began howling in pain. He dropped his pistol. As if on cue, Lewis triumphantly emerged from the woods, emerging like a black phoenix in military BDU camouflage gear.

The bow straddled his back. Reese's face began to show signs of happiness and elation as he walked toward us. However, her emotions soon transformed to fear when she saw Lewis with his arm covering the left part of his stomach. He was bleeding profusely from where a stray bullet from the mob had struck him. He was also limping.

This is the reason why the arrows ceased picking off the men one by one. It must have taken incredible willpower—fighting through the pain of the wound—for him to get off that last shot. With McGovern still caught up with his hand, Reese rushed over to Lewis and hugged him.

"Baby, are you alright?"

He slumped in her arms. "I don't know, Edith. One of those bastards spotted me in the trees and managed to get off a lucky shot before I brought him down. Sorry I couldn't be more help."

She kissed the side of his face. "Be quiet. You were there for me like you've ALWAYS been there for me."

Walking over towards them, I spied the two men by the tree. Indecisiveness and anger were written across their faces. This was fine by me. I had agony and larceny molded onto mine, along with pain and despair. I wanted to become a harbinger of death on a grand scale, killing someone until they died. When I got closer to Reese and her fiancée, I addressed him.

"Major Lewis."

"Dr. Mazique."

Reese was trying to hold back her tears. I could tell Lewis didn't have much time left to live.

"What's the play?" I asked.

He nodded his head toward the two men. "I will take care of McGovern. Can you take care of those two for me?"

Before I answered, I just had to have one more debate.

"Just so you know, house niggas never accost White people."

Lewis chuckled. "I never thought you were a house nigga. But you were the one who taught us in class to have the difficult discussions. I just think you believe too much in an ideal that doesn't exactly believe in you or your people the same way. You are a good man, Dr. Mazique: TOO good. You seek and see the best in people. But do you remember that bullshit book you had us read? The one by Bolman and Deal?"

"*Framing Organizations*?" I replied. "That wasn't bullshit!"

He laughed again and it was evident the effort hurt. "Whatever. Everything is an organization, but organizations are made of people who have egos. America is an organization, but it is comprised of humans who have egos: Some narcissistic, some opportunistic, and some racist.

"My point is that in an ideal world, someone with your beliefs would be a prime example of what we need. But we don't live in an ideal world. Instead, Black people need someone like me who will make the hard decisions and do whatever it takes to protect them."

Whimpering a bit, Lewis took his bloody hand off of his wound and reached into his pocket. He pulled out a white envelope which was sealed and gave it to me. For some reason, it felt as if he were handing me the keys to Pandora's box.

"Don't open this until you go back through the portal," he told me. I agreed with his last wish.

By now, McGovern, continuing to howl like a little—you know what I want to say—had come to his senses and was noticing his discarded weapon on the ground. Likewise, the other two men were starting to make their way over towards us. It was now or never. I wasn't going to deny Lewis his last kill.

"Are you sure you're okay enough to take care of him?" I questioned, seeing Lewis was having trouble standing up.

"I'm fine. Or, at least, fine enough to take care of this."

"Not that this is a competition," I sarcastically retorted, "but I bet you I will beat the brakes off those two before you beat the brakes off McGovern."

Lewis sucked up his pain and pushed off Reese. "You're on."

The lovers fussed for a moment about him going off to fight, but Reese knew her fiancée had to do this for himself. If he failed to take McGovern down, she would gladly deliver the coup de grâce.

I began making my way over toward the men. I bragged to Lewis, "This won't take any longer than

20 seconds!"

He started on his path toward McGovern and one-upped me. "I just need five."

As I passed McGovern, our eyes locked onto one another's. Though I was quite tempted to say something slick, I reframed. I felt he would reply with something dumb, which would cause me to strike him and steal Lewis' thunder. For his part, McGovern was still struggling with pulling the arrow from his hand and grabbing his pistol on the ground.

I worried he might reach it, but Lewis, though maimed, was making satisfactory progress toward him for me to continue to my two targets. The two men I faced were a pair of big ole' boys, each having about 10 to 15 pounds on me. Both looked younger and as if they weren't going to take an ass-whooping easily. This was fine by me. I wanted to see if I still had it.

Plus, knocking Cletus out had given me an extreme amount of satisfaction. I was looking to double down. Seeing I was older and it was two against one, the men thought I was easy pickings. Well, these two SOBs were about to find out I was from Missouri. I was going to SHOW them what a beatdown was by serving up a special can of unadulterated whoop.

"Coam ova hare!" one of them screamed. "We gonna bate yo arse, niggar!"

The great pugilist Mike Tyson once said every man has a plan...until he gets punched in the mouth. This fight was no exception. We both walked toward each other with no clear strategy, except taking each other out. They thought they would simply overwhelm me, but I knew the dictates of the streets and was pretty at good throwing paws. I determined which of the two men was the biggest and, at the last second, before any of us got within striking distance, suddenly pivoted towards him.

I stepped forward with my left foot and threw my jab with more power than needed. The punch snapped his neck upwards, setting up my overhand right. To hell with technique. When I hit him, I wanted his soul to leave his body! I swung wildly, cultivating the punch as if I had travelled all the way from Dallas, Texas. BOOM! The man ended up, unmoving, on the ground.

Five seconds.

"Who's the nigga, now, huh?" I taunted.

My other opponent's eye became as big as a milk saucer. He attempted to walk backward. I shot a quick jab at his ear.

"Where are you going?" I asked. "Weren't you talking shit just a second ago, too? No. Don't go anywhere. Come over here and take this like a man!"

Fear had seized my opponent, but I jabbed him again and convinced him to fight. This was probably a good thing. I was tired and wasn't incredibly fast. If he had run, I wouldn't have been able to catch him.

He turned to face me and swung off-balanced. I easily ducked and dodged his blows, punishing him with a barrage of body shots to prolong his torture, before ending it with a brutal uppercut that made him bite his tongue and sent him sleeping into the night.

Twenty seconds.

By the time I was through, Lewis had already completed his task within the allotted time. Hobbling up to McGovern, who had finally picked up the pistol with his free hand, Lewis had kicked the weapon out of his hand. When McGovern moved to grab him, Lewis—through sheer determination—had twisted and struck him in the throat, crushing his windpipe. This caused McGovern to react instinctively, grabbing his neck.

With the last of his strength, Lewis had lurched at the general, putting both of his hands on the arrow to force it into McGovern's throat. The two of them fell upon one another and died that way.

Five seconds.

By the time I walked back to them, Reese was hugging Lewis' dead body, consumed with grief. The wailing coming from her broke me down mentally and brought back memories of when my mother died. I knew the sound of that cry very well. Though it was not quite as strong as it had once been, it resurfaced in my mind from time to time throughout the years.

Hearing it made me understand the emotional turmoil Reese was going through. There were no words I could say, no solace I could offer. In the mind of the grieving, when one hears someone say things will be okay, it just sounds like so much blah, blah, blah. I overstood this, so I offered no words. I only offered Reese what I could at the time, two things I have always wanted to offer Black women: Comfort and understanding. I hugged her as she hugged Lewis and we both cried.

Chapter Seventeen
role reversal

Reese and I did not have any time to get caught up with emotions. We had a lot of work to complete before we could go back through the portal. The biggest thing we had to do was sanitize the whole plantation. This included getting rid of the bodies of the dead White men, along with Nguyen, Porras, and Lewis.

Reese is a badass. She compartmentalized what she was feeling—the recent loss of her fiancé—and moved forward the best she could. Perhaps it was her military training that allowed her to put her feelings on the back burner? Or did she simply do what Black women in America have done throughout centuries of hardship? Endure.

We buried Lewis further in the woods and quickly said some words. Yes, he deserved a better funeral service—as did Nguyen and Porras—but there was no way to provide him with one. I suggested we could take Lewis' body back through the portal and bury him in the present, but Reese had demurred. Lewis didn't have many relatives and those he did have weren't very close to him. Because of the nature of his work, he sometimes was gone for months at a time with no contact. Even she had bad problems, sometimes, keeping in touch with him.

Reese vowed to, one day, have Lewis' body exhumed and moved to another spot: This is providing his body was still there. Who knows what this area looked like in the present? In another century, commercial or residential developers might have discovered the body and moved it. Instead of telling her all of this, however, I said nothing. What did I really know? We had just traveled back in time. Anything was possible.

We untied Shirley. Since she was barely alive, we stayed a couple of days to make sure she was properly nursed back to health. But there was no way the feisty Yoruba slave could be held down for long. When she heard of the deaths of Clark and her slave master, she became jubilant and cried tears of joy.

Rounding up the rest of the slaves, Reese and I explained to them the situation. Too many White men had been killed for someone not to notice. There would soon be more coming to investigate. If they stayed, they risked being tortured for information or outright being killed in retaliation. Using maps and what I knew of the area and history of the time, I gave the slaves the best route North to obtain their freedom. Since the Civil War had broken out, escaped slaves no longer had to worry about fleeing all the way to Canada. They only had to make it to northern Missouri.

When the reality of their situation began to dawn on them, all the slaves turned on Cletus, beating him and savagely murdering him. Being a bootlicker helps one to accumulate a long list of enemies. If the slaves were going to run away and obtain their freedom, they didn't want a turncoat like Cletus coming along. It's not like I lost any tears over the guy. Up until the slaves killed him, he gave me the side eye every day.

He better be glad I didn't knock TWO of his teeth out instead of just one!

With the slaves' help, we retrieved the rucksacks and belongings brought with us through the portal. We destroyed them, hurling them into the forge of the plantation's blacksmith. I didn't want to leave anything from the present behind. We had already interfered and manipulated the timestream enough.

Shirley had grown curious about us and where we were from. As Reese nursed her back to health, she peppered her with questions about her life, about McGovern, and about Lewis. Reese answered what questions she could, but, understandably, had to deflect most of them and she felt bad about it. The two had developed an unusual bond and friends don't lie to one another. After much debate, we decided to tell Shirley the truth, that we were from her future.

Honestly, there WAS no debate. I learned long ago not to argue with a woman as determined as Reese. Even Satan would abdicate Hell rather than be harangued by her! Plus, I figured, what was the harm? It's not like Shirley would believe us, anyway.

And she didn't believe Reese, at least not at first. When Reese told Shirley the truth, Shirley looked at her as though she had consumed too much wolf water. Frustrated and desperate to let Shirley know she wasn't lying or drunk, Reese reached into one of her pockets and pulled out a picture she had brought back with her through the portal: A small portrait of Barrack Obama and his family in the White House. The President's seal was in the background.

It's a good thing I didn't know about the picture beforehand. I would have jumped Reese' ass for bringing something like that through the portal. Yet, when I later asked why she had done it, Reese explained it was imperative for her mental state to bring some form of hope back. The picture was symbolic of that, her protective shield, in an era of despair.

While I STILL don't know if Shirley ever believed Reese, I do know after she saw the picture Shirley once again broke down with tears of joy. Africans to slaves and then slaves to president? Who would have thought it? Shirley was head over heels with happiness.

Reese eventually left the picture with her. I had no knowledge of this until later. Though it went against the protocols of time travel, I didn't have a problem with it. Hope should never be contained, no matter in what form it comes.

***

To tell you the truth, I didn't know WHAT to expect when Reese and I went back through the portal. I only knew we had tampered with the timestream. Nguyen and Porras' deaths wouldn't have caused any problems. They were from the present. Timelines wouldn't be severed because they were no longer alive. But the dozen or so men we helped to kill in 1862?

Because of us, there were potentially thousands in the present who had been erased from existence. What if some of these had been destined for greatness? Destined to develop the next hottest invention? Despite our interference being something we hadn't been able to prevent, I couldn't ignore the fact it had happened.

If we had never entered the portal, the damage never would have been done. Regardless, I only expected to find a few subtle changes upon our return. What I DIDN'T anticipate were the not-so-obvious differences. The first thing I noticed upon our return was the difference in personnel.

Just so you know, the trip through the portal was STILL brutal, but since I was braced for it, this time it wasn't so discombobulating. Instead of my whole body feeling as if it had been assaulted by a meat cleaver, it was only my head feeling that way.

There was no one present from when we had initially gone through the portal. Maybe these people were from a different shift?

Yeah, right.

The next thing I noticed was the racial makeup of the room. Almost everyone was Black or another person of color. There was only one White person present and he looked to be of lower rank in the military. Before, the situation had been reversed. The last thing I noticed was the background and ambiance of the space we occupied. It was once an enormous room filled only with nothing but scientific machinery. It was still filled with scientific machinery, but now it was also filled with a myriad of balloons, several cakes, a dozen bottles of champagne, and hors d'oeuvres.

Forget all of the noise. I only paid attention to the food and the libations. In the back of my mind, I'm thinking, hell, yeah! I was so happy to be back home—and so hungry—I wasn't trying to notice anyone, anybody, or anything else. Regarding the new racial composition of the staff, I just figured the military was trying to promote a lot of minorities to fill a quota.

Except, this anomaly wasn't because of a quota. It was the new status quo. A tall, older Black man of some mass approached us as we were emerging from the portal. Music was blaring and confetti was being thrown around like welfare during a Biden presidency.

For some reason, I didn't think it was a Burt Bacharach crowd, but they could have at least been playing some Beyonce or some Sade.

Dressed in a suit and tie, the man stuck out his hand. He had an air of pomposity about him.

"Welcome back, Dr. Mazique! Welcome back, First Lieutenant Reese! My name is Dr. Darnell Williams, a graduate of THE Ohio State University. I'm the public relations officer for the military's Chronal Spatial department. I know things might seem a little different from when you left, but we assure you it's all for the best."

Who tells people where they graduated from when they first introduce themself? So, what, you were a graduate of THE Ohio State University?! I am a graduate of Saint Louis University. My school is so distinguished I don't need to emphasize "THE"! What's up with this guy and where in the hell is Thomas?

I saw Reese's arm begin to twitch, but she remained quiet. After all, we had been through, she had learned to trust me. Gazing at my look of compliance, she silently indicated she would follow my lead. Until we knew what we were up against, we needed to say as little as possible while at the same time trying to receive as much information as possible. I shook Williams' hand.

"I didn't know the military knew how to party," was my deadpan response. "Did we crash someone's birthday celebration or something?"

He attempted to placate me with a pseudo laugh.

"Of course, not. This is all for you two and the late Major Lewis."

Trying to dig for more information, I threw out a fluff response. "Really? The military loves us THAT much?"

Williams' eyes widened as he began to praise us.

"It's not just the MILITARY who loves you, it's the ENTIRE WORLD! You three changed history for the betterment of all people of color."

Uh-oh. Killing a dozen men changed the entire world? How? Surely, so small a number could not affect so many. There was no way!

"Before you debrief, take a minute to relax and celebrate with us! Everyone has been waiting for your historic return."

Though Reese and I did celebrate the festivities with the entire jubilant group, we did so reluctantly. We had failed in our mission despite everything we had been through. Somehow, however, Reese, Lewis, and I were viewed as heroes.

Everyone was carrying on as if the government had just given out reparations for slavery. At some point during the festivities, I snuck off with the excuse I had to use the bathroom. Though I did go to the bathroom, it was for a different purpose than relieving myself.

My intuition told me to read the letter, the Pandora's box, Lewis had given me. Luckily, there was no one else in the bathroom. I went to a stall, closed the door, sat down, and tore through his composition. What I read gave me a reason to pause. Fortunately or unfortunately, I came to understand why Reese, Lewis, and myself were being celebrated. I also understood how we had failed so egregiously in completing our mission. It was doomed before we ever stepped foot through the portal.

> Dear Dr. Mazique
>
> I write you this letter because I have a feeling I will not live to see the fruits of my labor. If that is the case, I wanted you to know I have immense respect for you. I believe in another lifetime we would have been fast friends. I never saw you as my enemy. We have too much in common.
>
> At the very least, both of us have passions for history and the betterment of Black people. We just have different perspectives on how to achieve the latter. You choose knowledge to

enlighten and motivate people to action. I choose to manipulate the timestream to give them an advantage they probably would never have. No pun intended, but I guess only time will tell which of us is right. Unlike you, however, I don't have the patience and faith in the *Keep Hope Alive* protesting rhetoric African Americans continue to espouse. Black people need direction and action and they need it, like yesterday.

I didn't want you to read this until after going back through the portal because you would have spent the rest of your life in the past attempting to undo what I have done, even though there was no feasible way to correct it. I know McGovern thought he was arriving in almost the same year and time I exited the portal. The problem with this is that I rigged the time machine. In reality, I came back to 1860, one year before the war started. I had two years to put my plan into motion before your group came out of the portal. Two years. For a man like me, who already had a plan put together when he ever exited, that is an eternity.

You have probably been briefed on some of my specialties. One is destabilizing governments. Tell me, how hard do you think it would have been to destabilize a technologically inferior populace? Especially in a country whose history has already been written and of which I have intimate knowledge?

I continued to read and the more I consumed, the more horrified I became. For a second, I had to stop reading altogether. I became utterly flabbergasted. Lewis had arrived in the past two years earlier than we had exited the portal. This meant he had plenty of time to alter the timestream. And he did...on a major scale.

Even the phrase, "on a major scale", does not accurately convey his actions. It was better to say, on an EGREGIOUS, major scale. Lewis had been right. Opening the letter before I went back through the portal would have resulted in me foolishly attempting to undo what he had wrought, though my efforts would have been Sisyphean. What Lewis had done was almost something out of a movie.

Skipping all of the details and getting straight to the point, he set up sleeper cells—amongst the free Blacks up North and amongst the population of slaves throughout plantations in the South—to carry out his plan. Yet the most audacious part was not the murder of John Wilks Booth and Andrew Johnson, Lewis' treachery called for the demise of over 100 enemies of the Black diaspora in America.

Hold on, Jim, there's more! Tell our gameshow contestants what else they won today!

While the sheer evilness of his plot overwhelmed me, I had to respect its magnanimity. What Lewis meant by saying I couldn't undo what he did was this: The assassinations would take place over the span of decades, well into the 20th century. Lewis had been more comprehensive than I had anticipated. Some of the people on his list hadn't even yet been born. Each member of the cell was responsible for eliminating anyone on the list who was alive during their time: It was also each member's responsibility to train someone younger to eliminate the people who were on the list during their time, and so on.

While not every cell would be successful in its mission—*one has to allow for shrinkage*—the sheer number of people involved would ensure a majority on the list were eliminated. In essence, Lewis set up a self-replicating generational set of assassins who would kill off the major enemies of Black people during successive eras. With 10 people in each cell, there were at least 200 people who started off doing his bidding. Lewis showed each person how to carry out an assassination, how to fire and aim a weapon, slip poison into someone's food, etc. He also left very detailed information on who was to be eliminated. No obvious historical enemy of Black people or perpetrator of systemic racism was spared.

This is why the personnel of the Chronal Spatial department project was entirely different. Lewis had totally rearranged the past! I scanned the names of the people on the list he had compiled and felt like slamming my head against a brick wall in an effort to offer repentance. Practically every target was a result of my conversations with Lewis. This is what made the last of his letter particularly hard to bear.

> I know you think I used you and the truth is that I did, but I don't want you to feel guilty or responsible for what I have done. If I hadn't gotten the knowledge from you, I would have eventually gotten it from someone else. I was THAT determined. Don't take what I did personally. It's what I do for a living. Someone had to strike before people like McGovern did. The only tragedy in all of this is I came to view you as a friend, even though in the end I had to treat you like an enemy.
>
> Lost forever in time
>
> Your frenemy,
> Major Darryl Lewis

Lewis hadn't taken much technology or equipment through the portal, but he did take videos and documentaries of history. He was able to play them on solar-powered laptops the military had developed. The videos served two purposes: To authenticate Lewis' claim he was from the future and to show free Blacks and slaves the potential hope the future held.

Having a background in psychological warfare, Lewis understood the power of images. He showed his recruits documentaries about key Black historical figures like Booker T. Washington, W.E.B. DuBois, Marcus Garvey, Malcolm X, and Dr. Martin Luther King, Jr. Even though Blacks would eventually obtain freedom, pictures of race riots like those in Elaine, Arkansas; Greenwood, Oklahoma; and Watts, California, were displayed and reinforced the belief that the struggle for equality and equity would never end.

Lewis ended his brainwashing of sleeper cell members by showing them a documentary about the Obama Presidency, juxtaposed with images of the January sixth Capitol riot. The resounding message to the recruits was that in the future, evil White men will gain access to a time machine and seek to undo all African Americans have struggled—through blood, sweat, and tears—to obtain. They could not allow that to happen.

This is the main reason he traveled back in time, to prevent the destruction of the Black race. Though it would be something esoteric to which they would be dedicating their lives, the act was more than worth their sacrifice. It would enable the continuation of the African American race and improve its condition on a grand scale.

Such a vision painted in the minds of Black men and women during this era made them zealously dedicated to Lewis' cause. When the time came, the sleeper cells executed his machinations with precision. And thus, history was horribly and irrevocably changed.

In Lewis' revised history, Abraham Lincoln was never assassinated, although Andrew Johnson died of some undisclosed sickness shortly after Lincoln's reelection, if you really want to believe sickness was the cause for Johnson's demise. John Wilks Booth was dispatched in 1864, shortly after he initially had hatched his plan for Lincoln, which was simply kidnapping him. An actor of little renown, nothing was thought of Booth's death, which was ruled a result of alcohol poisoning. Lincoln would eventually go on to serve three consecutive terms.

Because of this major time alteration, the **Hayes/Tilden Compromise** never happened and the federal troops did not end up leaving the South until approximately a decade and a half later than history had originally run. Since Lincoln was allowed to survive and Johnson was out, Reconstruction fostered far longer than it had. The number of Blacks in government offices and positions—already at historic highs during Reconstruction—increased exponentially.

This, in turn, opened up untapped social and political opportunities. As more positive aspects for Blacks increased, they also grew in different ways and in other areas. Academic achievement and pedagogy in the Black community surpassed anyone's expectations, ushering in a new social status. Blacks were able to gain access to and obtain better jobs. They became more than a complaining voice the government or society had to appease every once in a while. African Americans became a dominant force in society.

United States participation in World War I remained essentially the same, though Black participation this time was more lauded and racial restrictions for participation were not in place. Blacks did not simply dig ditches and do the grunt work. Unlike in the original timeline, African American troops fought alongside White American troops overseas and not with White French troops.

When Black soldiers returned home, there was no such thing as the **Red Summer of 1919**, the **Tulsa Race Massacre**, or lynching on a grand scale. But believe it or not, these were only subtle changes to history compared to what came next. While Word War II did occur, it played out completely differently. African Americans, who by now were

Republican and major players in government, led the charge for the United States to enter the war earlier than before.

For them, Hitler's genocide of Jews and insatiable thirst for regional domination was a sensitive topic that hit too close to home. Japan never joined the war. The United States had worked out an agreement regarding gas and oil reserves years prior to WWII ever beginning. When Hitler backstabbed Stalin and the Soviet Union on June 22, 1941, Black legislatures pushed for America to enter the war. Completely unprepared for United States intervention, Germany was forced to admit defeat three years earlier than before. Additionally, since America saw Russia's earlier nefarious alliance with Hitler as a bad sign of things to later come, it let General George Smith Patton run unchecked into Russia.

In the original timeline, Patton didn't trust Russia but was prohibited from pushing onward into Moscow. Of the Russians, he once said, *"I have no particular desire to understand them, except to ascertain how much lead or iron it takes to kill them. In addition to his other Asiatic characteristics, the Russian has no regard for human life and is an all-out son of bitch, barbarian, and chronic drunk."*

At that time, Patton didn't think it would take long to conquer Russia. He was right. Already reeling from the destruction of World War II, the country did not have the resources to fight and capitulated to America two years later.

This completely changed the power dynamic in the region. Another thing helping to drastically alter the timeline was the changing social structure of America. Because of the improved social status of Blacks, more people of color throughout the world immigrated to it. America became an even greater melting pot than before, eventually coming to resemble a salad bowl. The downside side to this—at least to Whites—was that they gradually became outnumbered and less in control.

For a time, America's increased global domination reduced the number of regional conflicts throughout the world. One result of this was that African nations became more united. America's diversity and ethnic progress were highly motivating examples for self-reflection and projection. Africans took notice of the rapid changes and improvements.

They followed the United States' lead. But then things took a turn and became something different and worse than before. While war is a bad thing, regional conflicts help to keep populations in check. This, in turn, ensures there are enough natural resources—like food and water—to go around. Unchecked populations help contribute to epidemics and pandemics because of the close proximity of the people.

The unusual period of peace throughout the world led to a drastic increase in the global population. Leading the way were Africa and India. By the time the 1960s rolled around, the world was already at 7.8 billion people, a population level the original timeline wouldn't reach until 2022. Ten years later, the first major wars started between Africa and India, mostly over resources. Though India had already achieved it, in the revised history of the world several countries in Africa also developed nuclear capability.

Both India and Africa used low-yield nuclear warheads in their assaults. Despite Africa eventually triumphing over India, it was a pyrrhic victory. Women and children were not spared. Millions of people perished and entire cities were destroyed. Disease and famine followed. China and Japan, both regional powers and rivals, sought to capitalize on Africa and India's weakened positions. Slowly, but surely, they increased their positions of power.

Yet, irritated and intimidated by America's audacious annexation of Russia, China eventually went to war with the American territory. The U.S. and China's conflict virtually destroyed Russia, with China also suffering more than a bloody nose.

While a peace accord was drawn up, an uneasy ceasefire continues to linger.

Adding to its population woes and disappearing natural resources, the world began experiencing new diseases and pandemics. Comparatively, the Spanish flu and Covid-19 had been mere colds in the original timeline. Over one billion people eventually died, mostly in Third-world countries.

The United States reacted viscerally—socially and politically—to the global crises seemingly occurring one right after another. The nation became more conservative and isolationistic. Eventually, it became an apartheid-like state. White people, no longer the majority and drastically reduced in stature, had their rights reduced and were made to live like second-class citizens.

By the time Obama because President, he was calling to *Make America Great Again*. Yet it appeared the only people who would benefit from this were people of color, not anyone White. Obama's aggressive nationalistic stance pushed the United States closer to the brink of war with China. His predecessor continued to do more of the same.

Meanwhile, talk of war, new diseases, and poverty throughout the world has interrupted global economies and job markets, which has pulled the U.S. into its THIRD Great Depression since 1939.

I didn't know how Reese felt about the new timeline, but after months of having virtually no contact with one another, she reached out to me. We were both having problems adjusting to our new hero status—which was a lie—and to the new world. While things have definitely improved for people of color in the United States, the overall changes have not been worth the effort. The world is in worse shape, more divided, and more ravaged than ever before. As I had told Lewis, nature would find a way to retaliate if the timestream were ever corrupted.

Understandably, the Chronal Spatial department was discontinued and decommissioned. Yet the machine is still operational and intact. Reese and I have come up with an ingenious plan to reenter the portal in an effort to restore the original timeline. We plan on going back to the exact moment before Lewis originally jumped through the portal.

If we are successful, things should revert to what they originally were. Next, we will take the evidence he had compiled against McGovern and make sure the general never takes a step outside of a jail cell, must less command any soldier again. The only problem with any of this is that Reese knows how her fiancé will react when we approach him, regardless if he is informed how his time changes will adversely affect the world.

We will end up killing him. Reese is at peace with this. She knows the Major Lewis we will encounter will not be her original fiancée, but one created by a deviation of the timeline.

I thought Marvel was the only one affiliated with a multiverse?

Yet the closer we come to achieving our objective, getting ready to step through the portal, one nagging, vexing question comes to my mind: If the roles were reversed, would someone White be entering the portal to reset history in African Americans' favor?

Come on, man, you already KNOW the answer!

Related Topics and Exercises

African-America Women

1. In what ways do societal norms and biases impact the treatment of Black women, and how can we work to dismantle those barriers and promote more equitable treatment?

2. How can we better educate ourselves and others about the unique challenges faced by Black women, both historically and in contemporary society?

3. What steps can individuals, organizations, and institutions take to create a more inclusive and supportive environment for back women, both in the workplace and in society at large?

4. How can we elevate the voices and experiences of Black women in public discourse, and what strategies can be used to ensure that their perspectives are fully represented and valued?

5. How can we address the issue of intersectionality, which recognizes that Black women face discrimination not only based on their race, but also their gender, class, sexual orientation, and other factors?

American Patriotism

1. Does standing for the flag automatically make someone a patriot, or is there more to being an American than just displaying patriotic symbols?
2. Is it possible to be critical of certain aspects of American society or government while still being a patriot and respecting the flag?
3. Is it fair to equate standing for the flag with being an American, considering that there are many different ways to express one's national identity?
4. Does the act of standing for the flag have different meanings or connotations for different people, depending on their background, experiences, and beliefs?
5. Should individuals be compelled or forced to stand for the flag as a condition of being considered patriotic or American, or is that antithetical to the principles of freedom and democracy that the flag is meant to represent?

Black Men and Black on Black Crime

1. Is Black-on-Black crime a result of individual responsibility or systemic issues?
2. Is blaming the police for police shootings deflecting from the issue of Black-on-Black crime?

3. Should Black men prioritize addressing Black-on-Black crime over protesting police brutality?

4. Is it fair to expect Black men to take responsibility for Black-on-Black crime when they face systemic oppression and lack of resources in their communities?

5. How can the community work together to address both Black-on-Black crime and police shootings?

How to Deal with a Racist

1. Should people be more willing to engage in conversations with individuals who hold racist views, or is it better to avoid interacting with them altogether?

2. Should there be legal consequences for individuals who engage in racist behaviour or speech, and if so, what should those consequences be?

3. Is education the key to combating racism, and if so, what kind of education should be provided and who should be responsible for it?

4. Is it more effective to call out racist behaviour publicly or to address it privately, and what are the potential risks and benefits of each approach?

5. How can we create a culture that promotes inclusivity and respect for all individuals, regardless of race, and what specific actions can we take to achieve this goal?

Ku Klux Klan and Hate Groups

1. Should the Ku Klux Klan be banned as a hate group, or should their right to free speech and assembly be protected under the First Amendment?
2. Is the Ku Klux Klan a relic of the past, or does it still pose a threat to marginalized communities today?
3. Should individuals who are found to be members of the Ku Klux Klan be prohibited from holding public office or serving in law enforcement or the military?
4. Does the Ku Klux Klan have a legitimate grievance or political agenda that should be heard and addressed, or are their actions and beliefs solely motivated by racism and bigotry?
5. How can communities and law enforcement effectively respond to the presence of the Ku Klux Klan and other hate groups, and what role can education and advocacy play in combating their ideology?

Reconstruction

1. Did the Reconstruction era actually achieve its goals of promoting equal rights for African Americans in the United States, or did it ultimately fall short?
2. To what extent did the Reconstruction era contribute to the ongoing issues of racism and discrimination that still plague American society today?
3. Was the Reconstruction era a missed opportunity for the United States to truly address and repair the harms of slavery and segregation, or was it simply an inevitable step in the country's evolution towards greater equality?
4. How did the different approaches taken by different states during the Reconstruction era shape the legacy of that period in American history?
5. Can we truly understand the modern state of race relations in the United States without a deeper understanding of the Reconstruction era and its impact?

Racial Equity

1. Should the government implement reparations for slavery and its legacy, and if so, what form should they take?

2. What role do affirmative action policies play in promoting racial equity, and how can they be more effective?
3. Should there be mandatory anti-racism training for all public officials and employees, and how can we ensure that these trainings are effective?
4. What role should the private sector play in promoting racial equity, and how can businesses and corporations be held accountable for their actions or lack thereof?
5. Should there be a national truth and reconciliation process to address the historical and ongoing harm caused by racism and racial inequality, and how can this process be effectively carried out?

Racial Harmony
1. What role do education and public awareness campaigns play in promoting understanding and empathy between White and Black communities, and how can these efforts be more effective?
2. Should the government invest in programs that promote cross-racial dialogue and relationship building, and if so, what should these programs look like?
3. What is the responsibility of White individuals in promoting racial

understanding and healing, and how can they best engage in these efforts without appropriating or minimizing the experiences of Black individuals?
4. How can we acknowledge and address the historical and systemic barriers that have perpetuated racial inequality and tension, while also moving forward towards a more equitable and just society?
5. In what ways can we promote cross-cultural exposure and interaction in schools, workplaces, and other social environments to foster greater understanding and empathy between White and Black individuals?

Teaching Slavery
1. Should elementary and secondary schools be required to teach the history of slavery in the United States as part of their curriculum, or should that topic be reserved for higher education?
2. How should the history of slavery be taught in elementary and secondary schools, and what resources and materials should be used to convey that information?
3. Are there any potential risks or drawbacks to teaching the history of slavery to younger

students, such as trauma or discomfort, and how can those issues be addressed?

4. Should the teaching of the history of slavery be mandatory across all states and school districts, or should individual schools have the flexibility to decide whether or not to include that topic in their curriculum?

5. How can the teaching of the history of slavery be used to promote greater understanding and empathy among students from different backgrounds, and what role can educators and administrators play in fostering those conversations?

White Extremism in the Military

1. What steps should the military take to prevent White extremist groups from recruiting and radicalizing active-duty service members?

2. Should individuals with a history of involvement with White extremist groups be prohibited from enlisting in the military?

3. How can the military better identify and address instances of White extremist activity within their ranks, including instances of hate speech, vandalism, and violence?

4. Should the military collaborate more closely with law enforcement agencies and

community groups to monitor and respond to instances of White extremist activity, and if so, what would that collaboration look like?

5. How can the military provide better education and training to its service members on the dangers of White extremism and the importance of respecting diversity and inclusion?

Creating Your Return to Nubia

If you could go back into the past to alter history so our society would be more equal and equitable for African Americans in the present, what would your course of action be?

1. Start by framing the discussion: Begin by stating the purpose of the question and clarifying any misunderstandings or potential biases that may arise during the conversation. Acknowledge that the past cannot be changed, but this question is meant to inspire a discussion about how we can work towards a more equitable future for African Americans.

2. Encourage historical research: To understand the impact of historical events on the present, it is important to conduct thorough research on the history of African Americans in the United States. Encourage participants to research events such as

slavery, Reconstruction, Jim Crow laws, the Civil Rights movement, and other significant moments in African American history.

3. Reflect on the impact of historical events: Once participants have gained an understanding of African American history, encourage them to reflect on how these events have shaped the present. Ask questions such as, "How do you think the legacy of slavery has impacted African Americans today?" and "In what ways have laws and policies been used to discriminate against African Americans?"

4. Brainstorm actions that could have made a positive impact: After discussing the impact of historical events, encourage participants to brainstorm actions that could have been taken in the past to make things more equal and equitable for African Americans today. For example, participants may suggest the abolition of slavery, stronger protections for civil rights during Reconstruction, or more aggressive enforcement of anti-discrimination laws during the Civil Rights era.

5. Discuss actions: After brainstorming actions that could have been taken in the past, shift the conversation to current actions that can be taken to promote

equality and equity for African Americans. Ask questions such as, "What can we do today to address the ongoing impacts of historical discrimination?" and "What policies or actions can we support to promote greater equity for African Americans in education, employment, and other areas?"

6. Encourage continued learning and action: Conclude the conversation by encouraging participants to continue learning about African American history and to take action to promote equality and equity in their own lives and communities. Provide resources and information on organizations that are working to promote equity and justice for African Americans, and encourage participants to get involved in these efforts.

An Interview with the Author

1. **Can you tell us about the inspiration behind *The Time Bandit from Nubia*? What led you to explore the concept of changing the past to create a more equitable future for African Americans?**

There are two parts to that answer. Believe it or not, actor Samuel L. Jackson was the major inspiration behind *The Time Bandit from Nubia*. I've always liked his work and the characters he portrayed, particularly the more eccentric ones. I started thinking about what I could write that would fit his character. Since I've always been fascinated by time travel, I explored putting him in a setting in the past, but I hadn't selected a particular era.

Then, I started thinking about how one of his characters would react if I sent him back to the Antebellum South and I burst out laughing. I imagined him using a ton of expletives, telling people to kiss his ass, and so forth...that is until the slave master's whip strikes him and then he begins singing a different tune. Only Jackson could pull this off! But then I started getting more serious with the plot and rethought everything.

What if I took this seriously? How would a

Black person from the present really behave if he/she were sent back to the era of slavery? How compliant would they be? *I would like for someone like Kanye West to go back to the era of slavery and see if it was really a choice. What a dumbass!* Once I had the basic concept for a story—a beginning and an end—I let the book write itself.

The second part of the answer is that several aspects of my life also influenced the plot of the book. I'm currently going into my third year of a doctoral program at St. Louis University. I'm working on an Educational Doctorate in Educational Leadership. One of the things SLU is really good at is pounding the issue of equality and equity into your head. *Like a sledgehammer. BAM! I mean, they never let up!*

Most assume schools in America are equal and equitable. *Give me some of that doophuny they're smoking!* But they're not. U.S. schools are some of the most unequal and inequitable in the world among industrialized nations. My cohorts and I are currently working on a dissertation that talks about equitable funding in Missouri public schools. But just as schools are inequitable, our society is inequitable. It's one of the things on which our constitution was founded.

Of course, there will be those who will debate this. *That's another part of the reason he wrote the book, chumps! You have something to say, write your OWN damn book!* Once I had the shell of a plot, I began playing around with the concept of equality and equity to add more meat. But the question enticed me to go down a rabbit hole, and it went deep. The result is this book.

2. How do you develop characters and how did you develop characters for this book?

Some characters are developed entirely in my mind, but it's best if I base them on something: Whether that is a historical character, one of my crazy relatives, or someone from my past. Once I set a character's temperament and emotional set—their personality—I simply place them in the setting of the story and the story writes itself. I don't overthink the process or try to control the narrative. I write where it leads me.

For instance, Dr. Mazique is a history professor who specializes in African American history and is very sarcastic and inquisitive. Whatever situation in which he is placed, his personality will always use intellect and sarcasm to control the outcome.

The trick with writing him is having witty commentary the reader finds interesting and funny, not corny and dull. His character forces me to think. But many of the characters and their names in this book are based on people I actually know. Dr. Mazique is based on one of my old mentors who are deceased, Attorney Dana Mazique, who was a professor at the University of Arkansas Pine Bluff when I was in undergraduate school. She was one of my political science instructors who really challenged me. Sometimes she would curse in class or engage in crazy political antics to shock us back to reality. She also challenged the male students about misogynistic views and strongly advised us on how we should treat a woman.

Her favorite saying in class was, *"A man has to make love to my mind before he makes love to my body."* I used to think she said that so the women in the class would realize their own self-worth. Over time, I've come to realize that perhaps she was directing her message to the males. We needed better direction as to what we should be presenting to women. A woman can have sex with herself. What else can you offer? The character is based off of Attorney Mazique. I just made her male and a history professor. The same attitude and wit she displayed in class are there.

First Lieutenant Edith Reese is based on one

of my colleagues with whom I work. She is an English Language Arts (ELA) teacher and has become my work wife over the two years we have been at the same school. When I arrived, it was my first teaching assignment since receiving my certification. I wasn't assigned a mentor, but Reese introduced herself and her help in the classroom has been invaluable. I honestly don't know what I would have done without her. Since I will be at another school next year, I wanted to write her character and personality into a story. There is no way possible I can tell her how much her help has meant to me. But there IS a way for me to show her. Words and books are eternal. I wanted her to always know I appreciated her.

Yet that's not the only reason why Reese is in the book. I believed she was a complex enough person around whom I could build a story. No, she's not an actual soldier, but the situations in which I placed her and how she reacted are very true to form. *I think she knows how to throw those paws, too.* It is funny how some things worked their way into the book. Reese's butt becomes a topic of discussion, and part of that is a running joke between us.

In my first year at the school, a male student commented out loud on how nice her butt looked as Reese walked by. While I reprimanded him, when I later told her about the statement, she burst out laughing. As I was writing the book and thinking about Reese's character and Black women during slavery, I realized her butt would have made her a prime target for rape. So, the running joke that worked its way into the book was really no joke. It was a travesty in the annals of American history.

Tony Porras was my Krav Maga instructor when I lived in Dallas, Texas. He is a second-degree black belt in Krav Maga and a Blue Belt in Brazilian Jujitsu. Porras owns a cyber security company and could probably hack into most security systems using only an Android phone. *Relax. He's a good guy. We're talking Dr. Mazique's level of ethics! Honestly, it's kind of annoying.* I don't know if he's necessarily liberal, but I do know he's open-minded and has dealt with his share of racism. He's normally quiet, reserved, and observant. But once he gets started, he will crack a joke with you or get into a political conversation.

He is in the book because his instruction and mentorship when I was going through a rough patch in Dallas really helped me to pull through. I've never told him this and I hope he reads it. When I called to ask his permission to use him as a character in the book, he just laughed and gave me the go-ahead. *Maybe you should have told him beforehand you planned to kill off his character. I mean, it's one thing to put the man in a book; it's another to kill him off!*

Dr. Darnell Williams was one of my mentors and professors at Langston University. He was a tad bit pompous but had the academic resume and intellect to back every bit of his hubris. He is in the book because he was one of the first professors at the school to show a dumb, young, freshman the possibilities and potential of his writing. Thinking he would live forever; I never thanked him enough his encouragement when he was alive. He received his doctorate from Ohio State University and always emphasized "the" when saying where he attended doctoral school.

When I used to ask him why he did this, he replied with a certain air, *"Well you HAVE to be distinctive. After all, there can be only one!"* I now know Dr. Williams was not necessarily unique in referring to his alma mater in this manner. From what I understand, ALL alumni of Ohio State University say this!

Lastly, the character of Major Darryl Lewis is based on a friend of mine who has been incarcerated for over 30 years. I wanted him to him know that he hasn't been forgotten.

3. **General McGovern's involvement in the mission raises questions about his motives and hidden   agenda. Can you provide insight into his character and what drives him to force his way onto the mission?**

General McGovern is one of the characters who is not based on anyone I know. Rather, he is a composite of all the angst and hatred of the mob who raided the Capitol building on January sixth. The statistics I quote in the book—20% of those arrested in the Capitol riot were current or ex-military personnel—is true. If this is the case, am I deluded enough to think someone like McGovern doesn't exist?

What drives the General is the fact he has something to hide and he needs to cover his tracks. While forcing his way onto the mission might lead to a military reprimand or worse, what he faces, if found out, will be infinitely more damaging.

4. **Without revealing any major spoilers, could you touch on the relationship between Dr. Mazique and Major Lewis? Does Dr. Mazique secretly hope for Major Lewis's success, and if so, why?**

Until he is contacted by the United States military, Dr. Mazique believes Major Lewis and he share a very amicable professor/student relationship. He relishes the debate and cognitive stimulation it provides. Since Lewis is not a traditional college student and is also an intellectual, Dr. Mazique views him with admiration and respect. But when the military contacts Dr. Mazique and he learns the truth about Lewis—well, what McGovern tells him is the truth—he feels betrayed and used. It's almost as if Lewis only got close to him so he could cheat on an exam, or at least that's the way Dr. Mazique initially feels.

While that's a bit of an oversimplification, it explains their relationship for much of the book. Dr. Mazique goes through the portal to confront his student. He's mad at him and he wants to know the truth. Their beef is like a relationship that went bad, where one person who doesn't receive closure goes on a quest to claim it. In theory, Dr. Mazique secretly hopes for Lewis' success but knows his plan will never succeed in reality. In fact, he believes it will doom reality.

5. ***The Time Bandit from Nubia* promises to immerse readers in the Antebellum South, with historical tidbits woven into the narrative. How did you research and incorporate these historical elements to create an engaging reading experience?**

It didn't require a ton of additional research. Most of the information I already knew. I write and publish a Black History for Beginners series under my birth name, D. Tyler Davis. I'm also a Social Studies teacher, so some things are second nature to me. If I'm writing about a particular era, I know certain elements from that time need to go into the book to make it believable. I have knowledge of those elements. Another thing is that my parents are from the South and I spent time there when I was younger.

My father's people were farmers and my mother's people were sharecroppers. Both grew up without any running water or electricity in their homes. Both picked cotton. Both told me stories of their childhood and both never let me forget from where I had come. What little I didn't already know was not hard to look up and analyze.

6. **What do you hope readers will take away from *The Time Bandit from Nubia*? Are there any specific messages or themes you wanted to convey through the narrative?**

We are living during a very violent, turbulent, divisive time. Everyone seems angry at something or at someone. Compounding matters are forces seeking to curtail different perspectives of history. I don't say seeking to control the truth because, many times, truth is subjective. What may seem one way to me may seem another way to you. But we do have a movement in America to limit perspectives of history. Why? Because somebody's feelings are gonna get hurt? *Sticks and stones may break my bones...*

There are multiple messages and plots throughout the story but the biggest message conveyed is for everyone to start having the difficult conversations and to stop avoiding them. Sure, America has an ugly past. *So, what? McGovern had an ugly mother! You don't see him crying about it, do you?* But I don't think that defines us, nor do I think it makes us weaker. I think it improves us and makes us stronger.

Bibliography

"The Most Terrible Ordeal of My Life": The Battle of Fort Pillow. (2023). Retrieved from battlefields.org: https://www.battlefields.org/learn/articles/most-terrible-ordeal-my-life-battle-fort-pillow

Anderson, C., & Wilson, A. (2021). *The Meritorious Manumission Act & Social Control.* Retrieved from YouTube.com: https://www.youtube.com/watch?v=jLky1i2GSH4

Andrew Johnson The 17th President of the United States . (n.d.). Retrieved from whitehouse.gov: https://www.whitehouse.gov/about-the-white-house/presidents/andrew-johnson/

Barnett, A. (2021, March 26). *From 9/11 to Insurrection.* Retrieved from bylinetimes.com: https://bylinetimes.com/2021/03/26/the-storming-of-the-capitol-part-three-from-9-11-to-insurrection/

Berman, S. (2022, March 30). *RUSSIA: Patton Was Right. Putin's Not the Problem | Steve Berman.* Retrieved from thefirsttv.com: https://www.thefirsttv.com/russia-patton-was-right-putins-not-the-problem-steve-berman/

Bitsoli, S. (n.d.). *Did Ulysses S. Grant really have a Drinking Problem?* Retrieved from historyisnowmagazine.com: http://www.historyisnowmagazine.com/blog/2017/4/3/did-ulysses-s-grant-really-have-a-drinking-problem#.ZF5s0C3MI1I=

Blassingame, J. W. (1979). *The Slave Community: Plantation Life in the Antebellum South.* New York: Oxford Unveristy Press.

Bolman, L. G., & Deal, T. E. (2021). *Reframing Organizations* (Vol. 7th). Hoboken, New Jersey, USA: Jossey-Bass.

Boucher, D. (2015, June 24). *5 things to know about Nathan Bedford Forrest*. Retrieved from Tennessean.com: https://www.tennessean.com/story/news/local/2015/06/24/5-things-to-know-about-nathan-bedford-forrest/29217861/

Brian Steel Wills. (1992). *A Battle From the Start: The Life of Nathan Bedford Forrest*. New York, New York, USA: Harper Collins.

Brown, A. (2021, December 14). *What Is The Meritorious Manumission Act Of 1710? How America Developed A Culture Of Snitchin' And Pro-Establishment Negro Leadership*. Retrieved from moguldom.com: https://moguldom.com/384864/what-is-the-meritorious-manumission-act-of-1710-how-america-developed-a-culture-of-snitchin-and-pro-establishment-negro-leadership/

Clingman, J. (2013, November 14). *Blackonomics: Selling Out and Buying In*. Retrieved from washingtoninformer.com: https://www.washingtoninformer.com/blackonomics-selling-out-and-buying-in/

Cobbina, J. E., & Huebner, B. M. (2003). Black Sexual Assault Survivors on Trial: The Intersection of Race and Gender in Legal Decision Making . *American Journal of Public Health, 93*(4), 582-584.

Debunking the Voter Fraud Myth. (2017, January 31). Retrieved from brennancenter.org: https://www.brennancenter.org/our-work/research-reports/debunking-voter-fraud-myth

Demby, G. (2013, July 1). *The Secret History Of The Word 'Cracker'*. Retrieved from npr.org: https://www.npr.org/sections/codeswitch/2013/07/01/197644761/word-watch-on-crackers?fbclid=IwAR2h0paTIEJoCdgx5SiYgrKkHcTV6w8zj3wKQrXqOGpbYXlidCXaVQidFDk

Douglass, F. (1849). *Narrative of the Life of Frederick Douglass, an American Slave.* Boston, Massachussets, USA: Anti-Slavery Office.

Feimster, C. N. (2009). *Southern Horrors: Women and the Politics of Rape and Lynching.* Cambridge, Massachussets, USA: Harvard University Press.

Fogel, R. W., & Engerman, S. L. (1989). *Time on the Cross: The Economics of American Negro Slavery.* New York, New York, USA: W.W. Norton and Company.

Foner, E. (1975, August). Andrew Johnson and Reconstruction: A British View. *The Journal of Southern History, 41*(3), 381-390.

Foner, E. (2011). *Reconstruction: America's Unfinished Revolution, 1863-1877.* USA: Harper.

Hernández, K. L. (2006, December). The Crimes and Consequences of Illegal Immigration: A Cross-Border Examination of Operation Wetback, 1943 to 1954. *The Western Historical Quarterly, 37*(4), 421-443.

Horton, J. O. (Ed.). (2004). *Slavery and the Making of America.* Cambridge, Massachusetts, USA: Oxford University Press.

Hunger & Poverty in America. (2023). Retrieved from frac.org: https://frac.org/hunger-poverty-america

Jacobs, H. (1861). *Incidents in the Life of a Slave Girl.* Boston, Massachussets, USA: Thayer & Eldridge.

Johnston, K. K. (n.d.). *From Craic to Cracker*. Retrieved from history-now.org: http://www.history-now.org/writings/from-craic-to-cracker/

Jones, J. H. (1993). *Bad Blood: The Tuskegee Syphilis Experiment*. New York, New York, USA: The Free Press.

Linder, D. O. (2023). *Celia, A Slave Trial (1855)*. Retrieved from https://famous-trials.com/celia: famous-trials.com/celia

Longacre, E. G. (2009, September 9). *Was Grant a Drunk?* Retrieved from historynewsnetwork.org: https://historynewsnetwork.org/article/42366

Matter, S. C.-H. (2011). *The Jefferson-Hemings Controversy: Report of the Scholars Commission*. (R. F. Turner, Ed.) Durnham, North Carolina, USA: Carolina Academic Press.

McLaurin, M. A. (1991). *Celia, a Slave*. GA: University of Georgia Press.

McWhirter, C. (2021). *Red Summer: The Summer of 1919 and the Awakening of Black America*. Norman, Oklahoma, USA: University of Oklahoma Press.

Moore, J. R., & Sullivan, S. (2018). Rituals of White Privilege: Keith Lamont Scott and the Erasure of Black Suffering. *American Journal of Theology & Philosophy, 39*(1), 34-52.

OPERATION WETBACK (1953-1954). (n.d.). Retrieved from immigrationhistory.org: https://immigrationhistory.org/item/operation-wetback/

Orlando, R. (2017, December 6). *'Silence Patton': First Victim of the Cold War*. Retrieved from Huffpost.com: https://www.huffpost.com/entry/general-patton-cold-war-russia_b_5526514

Patterson, O. (1982). *Slavery and Social Death: A Comparative Study*. Massachusets, Boston, USA: Harvard Universty Press.

Pfeifer, M. J. (Ed.). (2013). *Lynching Beyond Dixie: American Mob Violence Outside the South*. Chicago, USA, USA: University of Illinois Press.

Pfeifer, M. J. (2014, December). At the Hands of Parties Unknown? The State of the Field of Lynching Scholarship. *The Journal of American History, 101*(3), 832-846.

Reardon, C., & Vossler, T. (216). *A Field Guide To Antietam: Experiencing The Battlefield Through It's History, Places, and People*. NC, USA: University of North Carolina Press.

Scharping, N. (2020, October 17). *The Life of Genghis Khan, the Ruthless Warlord Who Created the World's Largest Empire*. Retrieved from discovermagazine.com: https://www.discovermagazine.com/planet-earth/the-life-of-genghis-khan-the-ruthless-warlord-who-created-the-worlds-largest

Schwartz, P. J. (Ed.). (2002). *Slavery at the Home of George Washington, Jr*. University of Virginia Press.

Seabrook, L. (2016). *Nathan Bedford Forrest and the Ku Klux Klan: Yankee Myth, Confederate Fact*. Nashiville, TN, USA: Sea Raven Press.

Seligman, L. (2023, 4 9). *DoD's highest-ranking trans official: 'Ostracizing anybody' will hurt military readiness*. Retrieved from Politico.com: https://www.politico.com/news/2023/04/09/ shawn-skelly-gop-trans-00090488

Shafer, R. G. (2018, October 17). *Trump called Ulysses S. Grant an alcoholic; here's what historians say about that*. Retrieved from newsleader.com: https://www.newsleader.com/story/news/his tory/2018/10/17/trump-called-ulysses-s- grant-alcoholic-heres-what-historians- say/1669699002/

Shmerling, R. H. (2023, April 17). *Is snuff really safer than smoking?* Retrieved from health.harvard.edu: https://www.health.harvard.edu/blog/is- snuff-really-safer-than-smoking- 202304172913

Steckel, R. H. (1979). Slave Mortality: Analysis of Evidence from Plantation Records. *Social Science History, 3*(3/4), 86-114.

Stevenson, B. E. (1996). *Life in Black and White: Family and Community in the Slave South* (Vol. 2nd). New York, New York, USA: Oxford University Press.

(n.d.). *The Trial of Celia, A Slave (1855): Trial Testimony*. University of Missouri Kansas City, Law School. Kansas City: UMKC.

Thompson, E. L. (2023, April 10). *At Fort Pillow, Confederates Massacred Black Soldiers After They Surrendered*. Retrieved from Smithsonianmag.com: www.smithsonianmag.com/history/at-fort- pillow-confederates-massacred-black-soldiers- after-they-surrendered-180981952/mpson

Tom Dreisbach, M. A. (2021, January 21). *Nearly 1 In 5 Defendants In Capitol Riot Cases Served In The Military*. Retrieved from https://www.npr.org/2021/01/21/95891526 7/nearly-one-in-five-defendants-in-capitol-riot-cases-served-in-the-military: npr.com

Wilson, D. (2021, Spring). SEXUAL EXPLOITATION OF BLACK WOMEN FROM THE YEARS 1619–2020 . *Journal of Race and Gender in Legal Decision Making, 10*, 122-129.